Welcome to Suite 4B!

Gone to the stables

Jina

Sssh!! Studying—
please do not disturb!

Mary Beth

<u>GO AWAY!!!</u>

Andie

Hey, guys!
Meet me downstairs in the
common room. Bring popcorn!

Lauren

Join Andie, Jina, Mary Beth, and Lauren for more fun at the Riding Academy!

And coming soon:

Andie held her breath as Katherine mounted Magic. The riding instructor gathered up the reins, patted the beautiful black horse on the neck, then squeezed gently with her calves.

Immediately, Magic spurted toward the rail, shaking his head from side to side. Foam flew from his mouth, and his eyes looked wild.

Relax, Andie wanted to tell him. *Katherine isn't going to whip you or gouge you with spurs like that nasty Mike Smythe.*

Suddenly, just as Katherine managed to slow Magic to a nervous walk, Andie heard a sharp backfire. Someone had started up one of the Foxhall vans.

With a snort, Magic wheeled around, throwing Katherine off balance. In the same instant, the van started quickly down the drive, shooting gravel behind it.

Magic reared, his front hooves pawing the air like a circus horse. Leaping forward, he headed straight for the railing at a wild gallop.

Andie gasped. Magic was going to jump the fence!

ANDIE
OUT OF CONTROL

by Alison Hart

BULLSEYE BOOKS

Random House 🏠 New York

"Do you think we should wake Lauren up?" Mary Beth Finney whispered to Andie Perez.

Andie looked over at Lauren Remick. Their roommate's head rested on a book, her long blond hair spilling over the pages. Her mouth was open as she snored softly.

"I guess so," Andie said. "We're supposed to be *memorizing* all the rules in the *Foxhall Student Handbook*, not sleeping on them."

The three girls were seated at separate tables in the cafeteria of Foxhall Academy, a private boarding school for girls in Maryland. Since it was only seven on a Saturday morning, the place was empty.

"Well, I can't blame Lauren for falling asleep," Mary Beth said, stifling a yawn. "Getting up at six a.m. is the worst."

"And it beats me why this punishment thing is called Breakfast Club," Andie said. Raising her dark brows, she scanned the empty tables. "Do you see any food anywhere? Or anyone else who's dying to be a member?"

Mary Beth giggled. "No. But you have to admit, except for getting up early, this isn't too bad for a punishment."

Andie snorted. "All we did was go outside the dorm after lights-out."

"Well, it *was* breaking the rules," Mary Beth pointed out.

Andie rolled her eyes. Mary Beth could be such a goody-goody sometimes.

"Ms. Shiroo might have sent us to see Headmaster Frawley instead."

"Frawley!" Andie snorted. She tossed her mane of dark hair behind her shoulders. "He's such a jerk."

"Andie!" Mary Beth sounded shocked. "He's the *headmaster.*"

"Who cares?" Andie looked over at Lauren. "Let's awaken Sleeping Beauty now." Picking up her student handbook, she threw it across the room. It sailed in the air, pages fluttering, and landed with a smack on the table in front of Lauren.

Startled, the petite blonde jerked awake. Her blue eyes blinked sleepily as she looked around the cafeteria. "What was that?" she asked.

"Your wake-up call," Andie told her. "Shiroo's going to be here any minute. We have to recite Foxhall Academy's three thousand student rules, remember?"

"Three thousand?" Lauren repeated, a puzzled expression crossing her sleepy face. "Are there that many?"

Mary Beth laughed. "It just seems that way to Andie. She's trying to break them all in the first week of school."

"Last night was a start," Andie said smugly. "Not leaving the dorm after lights-out is rule number—"

"Twenty-four," Mary Beth cut in.

"I knew that, Ms. Know-it-all Finney," Andie snapped.

"Oh yeah?" Mary Beth challenged. Laughing, she threw her own handbook at Andie.

Andie dodged the paperback as it flew across the cafeteria. It landed at the feet of Ms. Shiroo, the dorm mother, who had just appeared in the doorway.

"Oops," Andie said. She hid a grin behind

her hand. "Bad shot, Finney."

The dorm mother crossed her arms and gave Mary Beth a no-nonsense frown. Even on a Saturday, Ms. Shiroo was dressed in a crisp-looking blouse and skirt.

"Miss Finney," she said, "I hope this means you've memorized *every* rule."

Mary Beth's face turned white. "Uh, I think so."

"*I* know every rule, Ms. Shiroo," Andie said, smiling sweetly.

"I'm sure you do," Ms. Shiroo said. "Now, who wants to go first?"

All three girls raised their hands. Andie waved her arm eagerly. She wanted to get out of the cafeteria—fast.

Today the Foxhall riders were going to the Midway Horse Show, and she didn't want to miss it. Not that she was riding. Midway was a big deal, an A-rated show. Their other roommate, Jina Williams, and her horse, Superstar, were competing.

Andie didn't own a horse, and she'd only been in Foxhall's riding program for a week. She'd have to prove herself to Mrs. Caufield, the riding director, before she could show Ranger, the school horse she'd been assigned.

"I know the rules," Andie repeated loudly, hoping to catch the dorm mother's attention. It was true. In the last year, she'd been kicked out of two other boarding schools. They all had similar rules.

"Lauren," Ms. Shiroo said, "I'll start with you."

By the time the dorm mother had asked Lauren her last question, several girls and teachers had arrived at the cafeteria for Saturday's buffet breakfast.

"And lights-out is ten o'clock for sixth graders," Lauren finished. Her eyes darted nervously to the people filling up the cafeteria. Andie could tell she was embarrassed.

Swinging her foot impatiently, Andie ignored the incoming crowd. The horse show started at nine o'clock, which meant the last van would leave by eight-fifteen. Andie knew Lauren and Mary Beth wanted to go, too. But if Shiroo didn't hurry, none of them would make it.

"Andie?" Ms. Shiroo waved her over. Andie jumped up so fast her chair almost fell over.

"What responsibilities does a Foxhall girl have in regard to her classes?" Ms. Shiroo asked.

"To attend every class, hand in work on time, and study for at least two hours every night," Andie answered promptly.

Finally, after several more questions, Ms. Shiroo said, "You may go too, Andie. I guess you do know your rules. I hope you'll try harder to follow them," she added, but Andie was already heading toward the cafeteria door.

A few moments later, she leaped down the steps of Eaton Hall and crossed the grassy courtyard. Since it was still early, Foxhall's oak-shaded campus was quiet. Andie rushed past the library and under the stone arch that connected the library to Old House, the administration building.

The riding stable stood on top of a hill behind the school's academic buildings. On her way to the stable, Andie passed the indoor arena on the right and the two outdoor riding rings on the left. All three were empty. Most of the girls in the riding program were already headed to the horse show, either to groom or ride.

Andie paused at the last ring, imagining herself showing a beautiful young Thoroughbred. The riding program was the only thing about Foxhall that interested her. If she had to go to boarding school, then this was better than most.

But all these fancy schools cared about were their stupid rules. They were practically jails.

With luck she could get kicked out of Foxhall. Then she could live with her dad and go to public school. He was never home, and Maria, the housekeeper, was easy to con. Life would be one big party.

A shout behind Andie interrupted her thoughts. Mary Beth was jogging up the path.

"Wait up!" she called.

Andie looked back at the stables. A large horse van was parked in the drive. That meant all the horses hadn't left yet.

Leaning against a tree, Andie waited for her tall red-haired roommate to catch up. Mary Beth was just learning to ride, and she was still nervous around most of the horses. She'd never even been to a show before. Andie had no idea why Mary Beth had wanted to come to a school like Foxhall.

"Thanks for waiting," Mary Beth puffed. Her cheeks were red, and the freckles on her nose sparkled with sweat. "Lauren's right behind me."

7

Andie looked over Mary Beth's shoulder. Sure enough, their roommate was running up the hill to meet them. "I had to stop at the dorm," Lauren said breathlessly when she reached them.

She was wearing a white baseball cap, her blond braid stuck over the back elastic strap like a horse's tail. Like Andie and Mary Beth, she was dressed in jeans and sneakers.

"We'd better move it," Andie said, turning toward the stable again.

Suddenly she heard the roar of a van's motor. The horse van was starting down the drive.

"Oh no!" Mary Beth wailed. "It's going to leave us!"

"Not me!" Andie said sprinting for the stables. "I can catch it!"

Andie raced toward the van, but she was too late. It roared down the drive, passed the Foxhall Academy sign, and turned onto the main road.

"Great," Andie grumbled, stopping short. She glared at Lauren and Mary Beth as they jogged up. "Thanks, guys. If I hadn't waited for you two, I would have made it."

"Chill out, Andie," Lauren retorted. "We knew we might not make the show since we had Breakfast Club."

"I hope Jina won't be too disappointed we weren't there to cheer her on," Mary Beth said.

Andie crossed her arms. "Oh, that's right. Precious *Jinaki* got special treatment. She doesn't have to do her Breakfast Club time until Monday."

"That's because she's riding in the show." Lauren defended their roommate. "She needs points from this show if she's going to win the Junior Working Hunter Horse of the Year Award."

Mary Beth looked puzzled. "What in the world is that?"

"It means Jina wants to win a stupid silver plate at the end of the year," Andie explained.

Mary Beth sighed. "Well, I was really excited about going to my first show. I wish we could have had Breakfast Club on Monday, too."

Lauren shook her head. "You guys just don't get it. We were being punished, remember? The school doesn't care if we want to go to a horse show. But Jina's special. Last year she and Superstar won the Children's Hunter Horse of the Year Award."

Andie snorted. Jina was special, all right. A special pain. Just because she was a big-deal rider and had some super horse didn't mean she should get different treatment.

That was another problem with schools and their rules. Playing favorites.

Turning abruptly away from her roommates, Andie marched across the grass-covered courtyard. The stable was a horseshoe-shaped building with forty stalls shaded by an overhanging roof.

She stopped in front of one of the stall doors.

The top door was open, and a handsome bay horse looked out.

"Hey, Ranger." She patted his neck, feeling really rotten. It was the first Saturday of the school year, and they wouldn't even get to ride.

"You girls need a lift to the show?"

Andie swung around. Dorothy Germaine, the stable manager and part-time instructor, was waving from the doorway of the stable office. She was a gruff-looking older woman with short brown hair and a leathery complexion.

"Sure!" Andie said.

"Yeah!" Mary Beth and Lauren chorused.

Dorothy pointed to a beat-up pickup that had a cap covering the truck bed. "Climb in. I'll be ready in a second."

Andie ran toward the pickup. Mary Beth and Lauren met her halfway across the courtyard.

The truck's tailgate was already lowered, and the door of the cap was open.

"This looks like fun," Mary Beth said. She sat on the tailgate and swung her legs up. Lauren climbed in after her. Pushing aside a bucket, Andie found a place to sit across from them.

A few minutes later, the truck was bumping down the drive to the main road. Andie leaned back against the wheel well.

For the thousandth time, she wished for a horse of her own. She'd been riding since she was seven, but always on school-owned horses. She'd never had a horse she could really train, care for, and love.

All the instructors said she had potential as a rider. Andie knew that if she had her own horse, she'd work hard enough to go to big shows like Jina—and *win*. Maybe her father would even come and watch her.

Andie stopped herself. No way on the last part. Her father was too busy being the hotshot CEO of a big company to care what she did.

"And there will be some really top hunters at Midway," Lauren's voice cut into Andie's thoughts.

"Hunters?" Mary Beth repeated.

"You know. Those guys that shoot poor little animals," Andie said, biting back a grin. She couldn't help it. Mary Beth was fun to tease because she was so dense about horses.

Mary Beth just looked hurt. Andie wanted to kick herself. Why was she always so mean to her roommates? She just couldn't seem to help it.

After about twenty minutes, the truck slowed. Andie peered out the dusty side window as they bumped down a gravel road. The Midway show grounds were packed with horses and riders.

Dorothy steered the truck past a line of trailers, then turned and halted the truck beside two white horse vans that said FOX-HALL ACADEMY on the sides.

"This is so neat!" Mary Beth exclaimed. She twisted around, staring out the window on her side of the truck. "Look, there's Jina."

Craning her neck, Andie saw Jina mounted on her dappled gray Thoroughbred, Superstar, next to one of the vans. A half dozen other Foxhall girls bustled around them, leading horses and unloading tack.

When Dorothy finally opened the door of

the truck cap, the three girls piled out and ran over to Jina.

"You look fantastic," Lauren exclaimed.

Jina's dark hair was pulled neatly back and her cocoa-colored skin glowed. She was dressed in a black pin-striped hunt coat that cut in at the waist and flared at the hips. She also wore spotless white riding breeches, tall, shiny black boots, and a black velvet hunt cap.

Okay, Andie had to admit, *Jina* does *look pretty good.*

"Thanks," Jina said. "It was a good thing I was ready early. My class is first." She gave Superstar a pat. His mane and tail had been braided with blue yarn and his hooves painted with black polish.

Just then, a slender young man in his late twenties hurried up. "Ready, Jina? You and Superstar will need this warm-up class. The course is tight."

"I know, Todd," Jina said. "I walked the course twice."

Todd had to be Jina's hotshot trainer. Andie studied him. He had longish blond hair, a slim rider's build, and light blue eyes that darted from horse to rider to the show ring. And he was definitely cute.

"Class number three, Junior Hunter Warm-up, will now begin in ring two," the announcer blasted over the loudspeaker.

"Let's go watch the first rider," Todd said to Jina.

"Good luck," Mary Beth and Lauren called to Jina as she and Superstar walked toward the show ring behind Todd.

"Boy, is he cute," Andie said when they left.

"Superstar?" Mary Beth asked.

"No, stupid," Andie said. "*Todd*. Jina's trainer."

"He sure is." Lauren had a dreamy look in her eyes.

"Girls!" Mrs. Caufield bustled up, her clipboard in hand. "I'm glad you three made it." The riding director's gray-streaked hair was pulled back in a braid, and her eyes squinted from under a visor. "Lauren, I want you to groom for Myra Whitfield. She's riding Secret Agent. Andie, you can help Jina, and Mary Beth, you tag along with Lauren and watch what she does."

Lauren and Mary Beth nodded seriously. Andie groaned to herself. Great. She was getting to groom for Ms. "Special Treatment" Williams.

"I hope I don't have to hold Secret Agent still," Mary Beth said nervously. "He's so big."

"Don't worry about it," Lauren said. "Hey, there's Myra. See you later, Andie."

"See ya." Andie turned back to the show ring. Jina was still talking with Todd. Andie knew she wouldn't need any help until after her class. And from the number of horses waiting on deck, the class was going to take a while.

Shoving her hands in her jeans pockets, Andie sauntered down the drive away from the Foxhall van. Horses jogged past, the numbers on their riders' backs flapping. The show grounds were hot and dusty, but Andie loved being there. She'd be even happier when she got to compete. Maybe in a few weeks, Mrs. Caufield would decide she was ready for one of the smaller shows.

In front of Andie, several riders were warming up in the schooling area. It was an unfenced, grassy field a short distance from the show rings. Three pole jumps were set up in the middle.

She paused to watch the horses go through their paces. Suddenly, a dark brown gelding with a white star on his forehead caught her eye. He was big—over sixteen hands—but finely built and fit, like a Thoroughbred off the racetrack. Andie thought he was the most beautiful horse she had ever seen.

If only I had a horse like that, Andie thought as she watched the rider turn the horse toward the line of jumps. Suddenly, the horse's stride grew choppy. The rider reached behind him and cracked the horse on the rump with a whip. Instantly, the horse slid to a halt, then reared so high, he almost flipped over.

Andie gasped, as the rider flew off to the side. But he landed on his feet, just as the horse took off.

Head high, eyes frantic, the gelding galloped from the schooling area.

Holding out her arms, Andie called to the horse in a soothing voice. But he didn't seem to know she was there.

Out of control, the horse galloped straight for her!

"Whoa!" Andie yelled, waving her arms as she jumped out of the way. Confused, the horse skittered to a stop directly in front of her. Andie grabbed the flapping reins.

The horse backed away until the reins were taut. His neck gleamed with sweat.

Andie slowly walked up to him, holding out her hand. "Whoa," she crooned. "It's okay."

Just then, the horse's rider jogged up. He appeared to be in his late twenties and wore custom-made boots. A diamond-studded pin secured his silk choker.

"That sure was stupid," he snapped, jerking the reins from Andie's hand. "You could have gotten hurt!"

"Don't say thank you," Andie snapped back. "Your horse was headed for the ring at a dead gallop. He could have hurt somebody!"

"Not likely," the rider replied angrily. Spinning on his boot heels, he roughly pulled the horse around and strode away.

"Jerk," Andie muttered.

"Andie," a firm voice said behind her.

Andie turned around. Mrs. Caufield was standing behind her, frowning.

"That *was* a dangerous thing to do," the riding director said.

"But the horse was scared to death," Andie protested. "I was afraid he'd hurt himself or somebody else."

"I know, but it wasn't your responsibility to stop him. Sometimes you need to think before you act," Mrs. Caufield said.

"Sorry," Andie muttered, looking down at her feet. A sudden commotion in the schooling area made her look up again. Using his whip and spurs, the rider was forcing the horse to approach the fence again.

"I bet you'd never let us treat a horse like that jerky rider," Andie said.

"That 'jerky rider' is Mike Smythe," Mrs. Caufield replied. "He's a very well-known rider and trainer. But you're right, Andie. I never want to see any of you Foxhall girls punishing a horse like that. Come on, let's go over to the ring. Jina's jumping next."

Andie followed Mrs. Caufield through the crowd to Ring A. Lauren and Mary Beth were beckoning to her from ringside.

"Jina's jumping!" Lauren called.

Oh goody, Andie thought. But she was a little curious to see Jina and her wonder horse perform. Everybody always made such a big deal over them.

Andie squeezed next to Lauren and Mary Beth along the rail. Jina was steering Superstar toward the first jump, a gate with fake green brush on either side. Horse and rider met the fence perfectly, and Superstar sailed over it without a hitch.

"Since Jina's riding in hunter classes," Lauren explained to Mary Beth, "she has to jump Superstar over a course of eight fences that are three feet six inches high. The judge is looking for a smooth, even ride."

"They can't knock any fences down, right?" Mary Beth asked.

"Right. But in A-rated shows like this one, the competition is so tough that the horse can't even tap a rail or make a wrong stride."

"The ride has to be *perfect*," Andie added.

Silently, the girls watched as Jina and Superstar finished their round. Andie had to admit the two of them were good. Really good.

Lauren whistled. "No wonder Jina won last year's Children's Hunter Horse of the Year Award."

Andie snorted. "This hunter stuff is too tame for me. I'd rather watch jumper any day."

"Wasn't Jina jumping just now?" Mary Beth asked.

"Sort of," Andie replied. "But in jumper classes, the judge doesn't care about how you and the horse look. All they care about is who can jump the highest."

"Oh." Mary Beth nodded. "That does sound easier."

"Except the jumps can go up to five feet," Andie told her.

Mary Beth's eyes flew open. "Five feet! That's almost as tall as I am!"

"Look, there's Jina," Lauren cut in. She pointed to the exit gate. The girls ran over as Superstar strode through the open gate, and Jina dismounted.

Immediately, Todd, Mrs. Caufield, and several other Foxhall students crowded around Jina and Superstar. Andie slipped through and took Superstar's reins. She might have to groom for Jina, but that didn't mean she had to drool over her, too.

"An okay ride," Todd was telling Jina, a serious expression on his face. "You should have gotten closer to that second fence. Superstar was too bold."

Jina nodded. Her face was flushed and beads of sweat trickled down the side of her cheek. Andie knew that a great ride like Jina's was hard work.

"I'll walk him for you," Andie whispered to Jina.

"Thanks," Jina said.

Andie loosened Superstar's girth, then raised the stirrups and secured them by slipping the stirrup leathers through the irons. When the class was over, Jina was bound to get a ribbon, so there was no point in untacking the horse.

While Todd talked to Jina, Andie walked Superstar around for a while, then led him over to the Foxhall van. She took a rag from Jina's grooming kit and carefully wiped the dust from the horse's nostrils and face.

A few minutes later, Jina came over. Lauren and Mary Beth were tagging after her.

"I hope someday I can ride as well as you just did," Mary Beth was saying.

"Thanks, but it wasn't that good a round," Jina said. "I think Ashley Stewart on April Fool is going to get first." Bending down, she picked up a towel and wiped the sweat off her face.

"Ashley Stewart? Isn't she a Foxhall rider?" Lauren asked.

Jina nodded. "Yeah. And she's not real happy I'm competing against her this year."

"Well, no wonder," Andie said as she polished a stirrup iron with the towel. "She's sixteen and you're only eleven. She'll look pretty dopey if *you* win the Junior Hunter Horse of the Year Award this year."

The loudspeaker broke in. "Will the riders for class three, Junior Working Hunter Warm Up, please bring their horses into the ring in this order: number two hundred and four, number fifty-one, number one hundred and eight—"

"One hundred and eight—that's you!" Lauren squealed excitedly. "A third place!"

Jina sighed. "Just like I thought. Ashley and April got first."

"But you got *third* out of about forty riders,"

Andie said. She couldn't believe Jina was upset. She herself had gotten only one third place in her life at a small show—and never a first.

Jina gave her an icy look. "If I'm going to win the Horse of the Year Award, I've got to get first or second place. The show season's almost over, and I still need a bunch of points to win." Tears welled in her eyes. Hastily, she brushed them away with the back of her hand. "I have to win that award!" she added. "No matter what it takes!"

Andie jerked her head up, startled, just as Jina turned abruptly and led Superstar away. Andie almost felt sorry for her roommate. She was really stressed out.

"I'll never get that upset over *anything*," Andie muttered to herself. "Never."

4

"Poor Jina," Lauren said, when Jina and Superstar disappeared into the crowd.

Mary Beth frowned. "I thought third place was terrific."

"It is." Andie dropped the rag on top of Jina's grooming kit. "I guess it's not terrific enough for Ms. Special Treatment."

Lauren shook her head. "Oh, come off it, Andie. You heard Jina. The competition's really tight. And she's competing with all those older riders for that award."

"Would somebody explain what you mean by 'that award'?" Mary Beth asked in a frustrated voice. "And all this point stuff?"

"Okay, but let's get a soda first," Andie said. "I feel like I've been eating dust."

The girls went up to the concession stand

and bought cold drinks. Then they came back and sat on the ground in the shade of one of the Foxhall vans.

"Okay, Mary Beth, it's pretty complicated," Lauren began. "The American Horse Shows Association has a rule book that's over three hundred pages long."

Mary Beth groaned. "That's worse than the *Foxhall Student Handbook*. Maybe I don't want to know about showing."

"Sure you do," Andie said. "Then you can be just like Jina. Showing is all that girl thinks about."

Lauren frowned. "Would you lay off, Andie? Last week you picked on Mary Beth. Now this week it's Jina."

"And next week it'll be you," Andie said cheerfully.

"Come on, you guys," Mary Beth cut in. "Just tell me what Jina has to do to win this Horse of the Year Award or whatever it is."

"That's easy." Andie took a sip of soda. "She's got to beat out every other horse in the Junior Working Hunter Division in our zone."

"Our zone means all the different states in our show area," Lauren explained. She counted on her fingers, "Virginia, Maryland,

North Carolina, West Virginia, and Delaware."

"At each AHSA show—that's American Horse Shows Association—Jina gets points for every ribbon she wins," Andie added. "The points add up all year."

Lauren nodded. "And if she gets the most points, she wins the Horse of the Year Award for her division and zone."

Mary Beth had been looking back and forth from Andie to Lauren. "That's enough," she said, waving a hand. "I don't want to know any more."

"And she's riding against older girls because she won the Children's Working Hunter Horse of the Year Award last year," Andie continued. "She advanced to the Junior Hunter Division, where riders can be as old as eighteen. Of course, most riders wouldn't dream of winning the zone award in a harder division their first year. But Ms. Special Treatment seems to think *she* can."

Just then, Myra Whitfield rode up on a huge chestnut horse. Myra was sixteen and competed in Junior Hunter classes, too. She was a heavyset girl with broad shoulders. Her face was bright red from the heat.

Lauren jumped up. "Do you need help?"

Myra nodded. "Thanks. Can you hold Agent? I've *got* to get something to eat."

"Sure." Lauren took Secret Agent's reins, holding tight while Myra dismounted. Andie smothered a giggle. Myra's breeches looked as if they were about to burst at the seams.

A few moments later Jina led Superstar up. A yellow ribbon danced from the side of Superstar's bridle.

"Want a soda?" Mary Beth asked her. "I'll get you one."

Jina shook her head. Pulling off the third-place ribbon, she threw it on top of her grooming kit. "Thanks, but I don't have time. My next class is in half an hour."

Andie stood up and silently reached for Superstar's reins.

"That's okay," Jina said to her. "Todd's going to watch while I take Superstar over the practice jumps in the schooling area. If I'm going to win Junior Hunter over Fences, the two of us have got to do better."

Leading Superstar, Jina went off to find Todd. Then Lauren and Mary Beth left with Secret Agent.

Andie wondered what she was supposed to do. Finally, she went over to the concession stand and bought a chili dog. While she munched on it, she wandered among the horse trailers, checking out the different stables that had brought horses and riders.

The name Smythestead Farms caught Andie's eye. She stuffed the last bite of chili dog into her mouth and walked closer to a large, six-horse van. On the door under the name of the farm it read QUALITY HUNTERS AND JUMPERS—OWNER MIKE SMYTHE.

Andie glanced in both directions. No one was around. Curious, she strode over to the wide, open door of the van. The ramp was down, and she could hear a horse snorting and pawing inside. When she moved to the left of the ramp, she could see the horse's head peering out from one of the narrow stalls. The frightened eyes and star on its forehead told her it was the same horse Mike had been trying to jump in the practice ring.

"Hey, handsome guy," Andie greeted the horse.

He gave a low whinny, then tossed his head in the air. The chains attached to both sides of his halter jingled loudly, and his hooves beat an erratic rhythm on the wooden floorboards.

Andie frowned. The horse seemed so nervous. He never should have been left alone in the van. Suddenly, the horse lunged forward, and the chains jerked taut. Worried that he might pull away or rear, Andie started up the ramp.

The back of the van was sectioned off into three stalls, each about three feet wide. Luckily, the horse was secured in the middle stall, so Andie was able to stand safely in an empty one next to him.

"Easy, guy," she crooned. "You're too gorgeous to hurt yourself."

He pricked his ears at the sound of her voice and turned his head toward her. His eyes were wide and intelligent. But he was covered in sweat, and the floor of the stall was slippery with manure.

"You have to relax," Andie said, stroking his neck, "or you're going to hurt yourself."

The horse tossed his head again, then pushed her with his nose. A brass nameplate on the cheekpiece of his halter read MR. MAGIC.

"What a beautiful name," Andie told him. Suddenly, the horse threw back his head, then took two quick steps backward. His hind feet slipped in the manure, and he lost his balance.

His left side crashed into the side of the stall.

Andie darted down the empty stall and stood next to the horse's hind legs. Placing her hands on Magic's flank, she pushed firmly, all the while talking softly. The walls of the van's stall were strong, so she knew he wouldn't break them down. And there was no way she could push him upright. She just hoped her touch and voice would keep him from panicking.

Underneath her fingertips, Andie could feel the horse's muscles tremble. Then his back hooves scrambled for a better hold on the slick floor, and he heaved his hindquarters upright.

Andie breathed a sigh of relief. She hadn't realized how scared she'd been that he would fall all the way down.

"Hey! What's going on here?" an angry voice hollered from the van doorway.

Andie spun around. Mike Smythe was standing at the top of the ramp. Since the sun was behind him, Andie couldn't see his expression. But she could tell from the tone of his voice that he was furious.

Her heart did a somersault.

"You're trespassing," he growled, stepping closer. "I'm calling show ground security!"

5

"You'd better have a good explanation for being in here," Mike told Andie tersely. Stepping into the van, his eyes widened in recognition. "Oh, it's *you*. What are you doing in here?"

"When I passed by your van, I heard your horse going crazy," Andie told him. She took a deep breath. Okay, so that wasn't *entirely* true. "He'd slipped in his stall and was almost down."

"Hah!" Mike snorted. He'd taken off his riding helmet, and his dark blond hair was plastered to his forehead. "That's a likely story. My stable manager checked on Magic ten minutes ago. And he was quiet as a mouse."

"No way," Andie said. "Look at that horse. He's covered with sweat."

Smythe's eyes narrowed. "You're one of those Foxhall girls, aren't you?"

"What makes you think that?" Andie said, stalling.

"I saw you talking with Grace Caufield. So guess what?"

"What?" Andie asked, swallowing hard.

"I'm going to tell her I caught you snooping in my van." The trainer stepped closer.

Andie saw her chance. Darting around Mike Smythe, she raced down the ramp. At the bottom, she whirled around and glared up at him.

"Go ahead and tell Mrs. Caufield," she retorted. "I don't care. But I do care about your horse. Maybe you should, too!"

Spinning around, Andie raced away. Her heart was beating a mile a minute. She'd really done it now. She'd been rude and snotty to a big-deal show rider and trainer. If he complained to Caufield, the riding director would be *furious.*

When she reached the Foxhall van, Andie slowed down and looked cautiously around. Caufield was nowhere in sight.

She began to hunt for Lauren and Mary Beth. Then, out of the corner of her eye, she saw Mrs. Caufield in front of the secretary's stand. Next to her was a woman wearing a straw hat, white blouse, and flowered skirt. And next to her was Mike Smythe.

Andie gulped. If Smythe was talking to Caufield already, he must have been really mad.

The question was, what would Caufield do?

Suddenly, Smythe stomped away from the stand. The lady in the flowered skirt kept on talking to Mrs. Caufield. Andie figured she must be a show official.

For a second, her heart felt heavy. Then she told herself she should be happy. She'd been breaking rules right and left, trying to get kicked out of Foxhall. Well, she may just have gotten her wish.

"Hi, Andie," Lauren greeted her. She was leading Secret Agent across the grass to the shade of the van. Mary Beth was trailing tiredly behind them.

"Hi." Andie turned toward them. "So how's Jina doing?"

Mary Beth perked up. "You didn't hear? She won the class."

"Mary Beth," Lauren interrupted. She was hopping from foot to foot. "You have to hold

Secret Agent while I go find the bathroom."

"I do?" Mary Beth squeaked.

"Yes!" Lauren insisted. Thrusting the lead line into Mary Beth's hand, she sped off.

Andie rolled her eyes. Mary Beth was going to have to get over her skittishness around horses. The only one she'd go near was Dangerous Dan, her supermellow school horse.

Suddenly, Andie spotted Jina riding out of the ring. "I've got to cool off Superstar," she told Mary Beth. Her roommate was still staring nervously up at Secret Agent.

Jina halted Superstar in front of the van. For once she was smiling.

"I hear you won," Andie said.

Jina nodded and gave Superstar a pat. "Now we just have to win the other two Junior Hunter classes."

Andie reached for the reins. "I'll untack him."

"Thanks." Jina dismounted, then dropped down on the grass to pull off her boots. Andie unbuckled Superstar's girth, slid off the saddle, and leaned it against the van tire.

She had just finished unbuckling the throatlatch when Mrs. Caufield came up. The director's cheeks were flushed and her lips were pressed together tightly.

Andie's heart flip-flopped.

"Andie," Mrs. Caufield said, with a gaze like a drill sergeant's. "I need to talk to you."

This is it, Andie told herself. *This is where she tells me I'm being kicked out of Foxhall Academy.*

Suddenly a scream pierced the air. "Runaway horse!" Mary Beth called.

Andie and Mrs. Caufield whirled around. Secret Agent was ambling across the grass, his lead line dragging on the ground. Mary Beth darted back and forth behind him, flapping her arms like a bird.

Andie couldn't help it. She cracked up. So did Jina.

Mrs. Caufield hitched in her breath. "Honestly!" the director muttered. "I'll speak with *you* later," she said to Andie, then she walked briskly over to Agent and grabbed his dangling lead line. Andie breathed a huge sigh of relief. Saved—for now.

Later that afternoon, Andie watched Jina trot Superstar into the jumping ring. This was their last class. And Jina was tied for the Midway Junior Hunter Championship with Ashley Stewart. Ashley and her horse, April Fool, had just finished a beautiful round. Jina and Superstar would have to be perfect to beat them.

"I know they can do it," Lauren whispered to Andie. The fingers of both her hands were crossed as she leaned over the fence rail. Mary Beth stood next to her, a tense look on her dirt-streaked face.

Jina cantered Superstar toward the gate. Ears pricked, eyes alert, he flew effortlessly over every obstacle. When he sailed over the last fence, loud applause broke out around the ring.

"They did it!" Lauren and Mary Beth squealed as they hugged each other. "A perfect round!"

Five minutes later, the loudspeaker announced the results. "Will riders for class number twenty-two, Junior Hunter over Fences, please enter the ring at a jog—number one hundred and eight, number—"

"Wow! First place! She really *did* do it," Andie said.

"Since she won that class, does she win the Junior Hunter Championship for the show?" Mary Beth asked.

Andie nodded. "Yes. At the end of the show, she'll get a big tricolored ribbon and trophy. For winning the class, she'll get a blue ribbon."

"Andie," Mrs. Caufield called.

Andie spun around. The riding director was striding toward her, a lead line in her hand.

"Yes?" Andie asked hesitantly. In all the excitement over Jina, she'd almost forgotten about Mike Smythe and his horse. Obviously, Mrs. Caufield had not.

Andie steeled herself for the big lecture.

"I need your help," the director said.

Help? "Uh, sure," Andie stammered.

Mrs. Caufield walked briskly toward a row of vans on the other side of the show grounds. Andie jogged beside her, trying to keep up. She had no idea what was going on.

Soon she realized they were headed for Mike Smythe's van. The woman in the flowered skirt was standing at the end of the ramp.

Andie's heart sank. Uh-oh. If the woman *was* a show official, she might be in major trouble after all.

But Mike Smythe was nowhere in sight.

"I do suppose this is the best thing to do," the woman said when Andie and Mrs. Caufield came up. She was wringing her hands, and her face looked worried.

Andie stopped at the end of the ramp. What's going on? she wanted to ask, but the two women ignored her. She peeked into the van. Magic bobbed his head at her nervously.

"It is the right thing to do, Marian," the director replied. "You need to get him off the show circuit. He needs lots of patient schooling."

Were they talking about Magic? Andie wondered.

"I've had three different trainers work with him this past year," the woman in the flowered skirt said. Her gaze darted worriedly to Magic.

"True," Mrs. Caufield replied, "but he's only gotten worse. Mike may be the best, but he obviously doesn't have the time to devote to this horse's particular problems."

"Excuse me," Andie said in her most polite voice. "But are you talking about Magic?"

Mrs. Caufield turned around. "Yes," she replied. "We're taking Mr. Magic back to school with us."

Andie caught her breath.

She couldn't believe it! *Magic was coming to Foxhall!*

6

"You're right, Andie, Magic is really gorgeous," Lauren said the next day. She was sitting next to Andie on the top rail of Foxhall's back pasture. Jina and Mary Beth were on either side of them, watching the horse prance cautiously around the grassy field.

"And look at the way he moves," Andie said excitedly. "Smooth, graceful, with a powerful stride. It's so great he's here."

Right after Sunday breakfast, the four roommates had run up to the stables to see Magic.

The horse suddenly bolted sideways as a leaf blew into the air.

Jina shook her head. "He *is* beautiful, but he sure spooks a lot."

"Do you think something's wrong with

40

him?" Mary Beth asked. "It took you guys an hour to load him into the van yesterday."

"Something's wrong all right," Andie replied. "Mrs. Caufield said Magic had an accident in a trailer last year. The trailer flipped onto its side, with him in it. He wasn't injured, but it totally freaked him out."

"Besides, Thoroughbreds are very high-strung," Jina added. "I still wonder why a professional like Mike Smythe couldn't do anything with him, though."

"That jerk?" Andie snorted. "He might be some hotshot trainer, but he doesn't know how to handle sensitive horses. You just wait. I'm going to get Caufield to assign Magic to *me*."

"Oh, come off it, Andie," Lauren scoffed. "There's no way *you* could handle Magic."

Just then Dorothy Germaine came up to the gate leading Three Bars Jake, a chunky quarter horse.

"Let's see if some company will help calm Magic down," the stable manager said.

When Magic saw Jake, his head popped high and his ears tilted forward. Dorothy opened the gate and unhooked the lead line from Jake's halter. The quarter horse took two steps, stopped, and started grazing.

Magic stared at Jake as if he'd never seen another horse before. Neck arched, nostrils flared, he slowly approached.

Dorothy made a *tsk*ing noise in her throat. "I don't think that animal will ever make a good school horse."

"Then why is he here?" Lauren asked.

"Because Mrs. Caufield can tell he's special," Andie said quickly.

"Not exactly," Dorothy replied. "His owner donated him to Foxhall, and he *is* a beauty. I guess Mrs. Caufield didn't want to turn him down. Katherine Parks is going to try him out after lunch, so we'll see how it goes."

Andie's eyes widened. "Can we watch?"

Dorothy frowned. "I don't know. You'd better get permission first. Now do me a favor and keep your eyes on his highness here. Holler if anything goes wrong."

The four girls nodded. As soon as Dorothy left, Andie turned her attention back to Magic. He'd taken about ten steps toward Jake. She smiled as his expression changed from fearful to curious.

"Well, I sure want to watch when Katherine rides him," Lauren said.

"Me too," Andie said. Katherine Parks, the

42

dressage instructor, was a super rider. What could possibly go wrong?

"Do you think this meat is from some kind of animal we've never heard of?" Lauren asked Andie at lunch. The two girls were standing in the food line in the cafeteria. Lauren was staring down at a tray of cold cuts.

"That stuff's from a pink turkey," Andie said, pointing at a row of deli meat. "Haven't you ever seen them at Easter?"

Lauren gave her a funny look.

"That stuff does look suspicious," Mary Beth said over Lauren's shoulder.

Lauren wrinkled her nose. "Maybe I'll become a vegetarian."

Andie glanced around the cafeteria. All the girls were dressed in shorts. Since most of the faculty ate at their homes or off campus on the weekends and many of the students were away on weekend passes, Sunday meals were informal.

"So where's Ms. Junior Hunter Champion?" Andie asked, looking for Jina.

Lauren headed over to the salad bar. "She met Todd back at the dorm in the common room. He videotaped one of Jina's classes at yesterday's show, and he wanted to go over every second of it."

Andie blew a stray strand of hair from her forehead. "How boring," she said as she plopped some salad in her bowl.

"Oh, I wouldn't mind watching a video with Todd. He's so cute." Lauren sighed. "He's wearing this cool denim shirt and his hair is all blond and curly."

Andie snorted. "Oh, give me a break, Lauren. Todd's got to be in his twenties."

"So?" Lauren looked offended.

"*So* have you even gone on a date before?" Andie challenged. "With anyone?"

Lauren flushed.

"That's what I thought." Andie tossed the salad tongs back into the bowl and picked up her tray.

She spotted Mary Beth in a corner. On weekends they didn't have assigned tables.

Mary Beth was shoveling steaming globs of meat and potatoes into her mouth.

"That's gross," Andie said as she sat down.

Mary Beth ignored her.

"So have *you* ever been on a date before, Ms. Know-it-all?" Lauren asked, coming up behind Andie. She dropped her tray next to Andie's with a loud clunk.

Mary Beth stopped eating. "Did I miss something here?"

Andie shook her head. "Lauren was just drooling over Todd. And, yes, I've been on *tons* of dates."

Mary Beth looked puzzled. "Todd? Aren't he and Jina watching that videotape from the show?"

Andie grinned. "Yeah. Only Lauren wishes she was with him instead."

"Oh, shut up, Andie." Lauren pulled out her chair, scraping it noisily along the tiles. "I just said I thought he was cute. And I've been on tons of dates, too. So there."

"You have?" Mary Beth asked eagerly, her green eyes lighting up.

"Yeah? When?" Andie speared her fork into her lettuce.

"Ummm." Lauren busily unfolded her napkin and spread it over her lap. "I went with a guy to the sixth grade dance at the school I used to go to."

Andie stopped chewing. "The *sixth* grade dance? We're in sixth grade now."

Flushing red, Lauren froze in her seat. "I didn't mean *sixth* grade."

"What's the matter, Remick?" Andie challenged. "Are you repeating sixth grade this year at Foxhall?"

Tears filled Lauren's eyes.

Mary Beth shot Andie an angry look. "So what if she is?"

Andie shrugged, feeling embarrassed. She hadn't meant to make Lauren cry. "I just wondered. I mean, you're so short, Lauren, I figured you were our age." Looking down at her salad, Andie stuffed a wad of lettuce in her mouth.

Lauren sniffed and stared down at her plate.

"And I haven't been on *tons* of dates," Andie added, trying to make her roommate feel better.

When Lauren didn't respond, Andie glanced up at the clock on the cafeteria wall. It was almost twelve-thirty.

"Uh-oh. We'd better hurry if we want to see Katherine ride Magic," she said.

"Jina told me she'll meet us there," Mary Beth said. "Todd wants to watch, too."

"Oooo, *Todd*." Andie nudged Lauren. Her

blond roommate smiled weakly. Then Mary Beth started laughing, until finally Lauren couldn't help but join in.

Half an hour later the roommates lined up along the railing of the riding ring located below the stable. Todd stood in the middle.

"Isn't he gorgeous?" Lauren said.

"Do you think she means Magic or Todd?" Andie whispered to Mary Beth.

Jina turned and looked at them as though they were crazy. Lauren glared at them, too. "Will you guys shut up!" she hissed.

"Girls!" Mrs. Caufield's voice boomed over the ring. "If you're going to watch, you'll have to be quiet."

She held Magic's reins while Katherine zipped up her leather chaps. The horse looked around nervously, then lurched forward, almost stomping on the director's toes.

Andie crossed her fingers and held her breath as Katherine mounted. The instructor gathered up her reins, patted Magic soothingly on the neck, then squeezed gently with her calves.

Spurting forward, Magic jigged toward the rail. Foam flew from his mouth as he shook his head from side to side.

Relax, Andie wanted to tell him. She's not going to whip you like that nasty Mike Smythe.

By the time horse and rider reached the railing, Katherine had slowed Magic to a nervous walk.

Suddenly there was a sharp backfire from the other side of the ring. Someone had started up one of the horse vans, Andie realized.

With a snort, Magic wheeled completely around, throwing Katherine off balance. At the same instant, the van rumbled down the drive, shooting gravel behind it.

Startled by the noise, Magic reared, his front hooves pawing the air like a circus horse. Leaping forward, he headed straight for the railing at a wild gallop.

Andie gasped. He was going to jump the fence!

7

"Magic, whoa!" Andie cried.

Magic slid to a stop. Katherine flew onto his neck, straddled it for an instant, then fell to the ground.

Immediately, the instructor jumped to her feet unhurt. Magic spun in a semicircle and raced away, his eyes wide with fear.

Andie climbed quickly over the fence. She had to stop Magic before he hurt himself!

Magic galloped toward the closed gate, then veered to the left. Nostrils flaring, he snorted, slowed to a trot, then halted.

Andie approached him slowly from the right, talking quietly. "Hey, guy, are you okay? Did that van frighten you?"

Without turning his head, Magic flicked an ear toward her. His sides were heaving and his legs trembled as Andie drew closer.

But when she reached out to scoop up the reins, he shied sideways. Andie touched his neck, then ran her hand down his legs. He seemed to be okay.

Andie looked back toward the other side of the ring. Jina, Mary Beth, Todd, and Lauren were crowded against the fence, watching her anxiously. Katherine was brushing off her chaps. And Mrs. Caufield was marching across the ring toward Andie, her lips pressed in a thin line.

"Uh-oh," Andie muttered to Magic. "It doesn't look good—for either of us."

"Grace, wait!" Katherine called, jogging after the director. "I want to try him again."

"No way," Mrs. Caufield replied without breaking stride.

"He was just scared," Katherine said when she caught up with the director. "We can take it slower."

Mrs. Caufield shook her head. "I knew that horse was high-strung. I didn't realize he was crazy."

Crazy! Andie gulped and her fingers tensed on the reins. That didn't sound good at all!

"He's not crazy," Katherine said. "He's light

and sensitive, and I think he'll make a terrific horse. It might be good for some of the girls to get experience working with a green horse," she added.

The two women stopped in front of Andie.

"You could assign Magic to me," Andie blurted out. "I mean, not to ride right away, but I could groom him and—"

"Andie's right," Katherine cut in. "Magic needs one person to spend time with him to build up his trust."

Mrs. Caufield studied Magic. For once, he was standing quietly, his muzzle against Andie's shoulder.

Finally the director said, "All right, Andie. If anyone can handle Magic, you can. I'll give you two weeks."

"Yes!" Andie exclaimed gleefully.

"But don't you get on that horse." She shook her finger in warning. "You'll continue to ride Ranger. Do you hear me, Ms. Perez?"

Andie nodded solemnly. But when the director turned and walked away, she started to grin excitedly. *Magic had another chance!*

"Rob Robertson is *so* gorgeous," Lauren said when the lights in the auditorium flicked on.

It was Sunday evening, and the four roommates had just finished watching a horror movie in the Foxhall auditorium. Scattered around the room were about twenty other students of all ages.

"Yeah. I'd share a pizza with him any day," Mary Beth agreed. Yawning, she stretched her long legs into the aisle.

Jina was still leaning back in her seat, staring up at the blank screen. "I kind of like James Douglas better than Rob Robertson," she said. "He's cuter."

Andie hardly heard them. She was slouched down in her seat finishing the last of her popcorn.

"Earth to Andie," Mary Beth said.

"Hmmm?" Andie looked up. All three of her roommates were staring at her. "Is the movie over?"

"Yes, dummy," Lauren teased. "That's why they turned the lights on."

"Oh." Andie jumped up, and the seat of the chair *spronged* upright. "Are you ready to go?"

Lauren, Mary Beth, and Jina exchanged puzzled glances. Mary Beth reached over and put her hand on Andie's forehead.

"Are you sick?" she asked.

Andie knocked her hand away. "No. Why are you asking a stupid question like that?"

Jina cocked her head. "Because you were so quiet through the whole movie. No whistles, catcalls—"

"And you didn't once say—" standing up, Lauren stuck out one hip and tossed her hair behind her ears, imitating Andie—"'Ooo, Lauren, they're kissing. Don't you wish that was you and Todd?'"

Jina and Mary Beth burst into giggles. Andie rolled her eyes. Her roommates were such babies.

"Grow up, guys. I've got better things to think about." Turning, she stepped over Jina's legs and made her way into the aisle. By the time she reached the exit, Jina, Lauren, and Mary Beth were right behind her.

"*Better* things?" Mary Beth asked. "Like what? Getting kicked out of Foxhall? Seems to me you haven't been working on that very hard lately."

"That's because it's the weekend," Andie shot over her shoulder. "Besides, I can't get kicked out right now. I'm going to be working with Magic, remember?"

"Magic? Why are you so nuts about that

horse?" Lauren asked as Andie pushed open the heavy double doors.

Andie shrugged. "I don't know." She turned to Jina. "You're a hotshot rider, Williams. What do *you* think Magic's problem is?"

For a second, Jina looked surprised. Then she answered, "I don't know. I've always ridden well-trained horses."

"Then how about you, Lauren?" Andie asked as the four of them went down the steps. "What would you do?"

"I've never ridden a green horse, either," Lauren replied. "Except when I was younger, we did have a pony that bucked us off a lot."

"So what did you do with him?" Andie persisted.

Lauren shrugged. "Sold him. Now my parents just have mares and foals."

"Oh great. So nobody knows what to do with Magic?" Andie asked, feeling frustrated. She stopped under the stone arch that linked Old House to the library.

Her three roommates shook their heads. Then Mary Beth said, "Why don't you pretend *you're* a horse that's scared and think how you'd like to be handled?"

Andie snorted. "That's a dumb idea."

Mary Beth looked hurt.

"At least she *had* an idea," Lauren retorted. "Come on. We'd better head back to the dorm. It's almost eight o'clock. Who would have thought we'd have mandatory study time on Sunday nights?"

Jina sighed. "At least it's only an hour. And I have to go to bed early. I've got Breakfast Club tomorrow."

"Yuck." Mary Beth made a face. "Now I'm glad we got our punishment over with."

"And don't forget room inspection after breakfast," Lauren added as they started walking again.

"I'll see you guys later," Andie said. "I'm not going in yet."

"Don't be late for curfew," Jina told her. "Or you'll be stuck in Breakfast Club with me in the morning."

Andie nodded, then shoved her hands in the pockets of her shorts and watched as her roommates disappeared through the double doors of Bracken Hall. With a sigh, she sat on the stone bench under the arch.

Curfew, study hours, room inspection—rules, rules.

She was so sick of them.

And what really made her mad was the fact that Caufield was only giving Magic two weeks. If only Magic were really her horse. Then she could take as much time as she needed with him. Not that she knew what to do.

Pretend you're a horse that's scared, Mary Beth had said.

Leaning back against the trellis, Andie squeezed her eyes shut. If she were Magic, she'd want someone to brush her gently every day, then take her for long walks to check out all the spooky things in the world. She'd want someone to explain to her what all those spooky things were and why they couldn't hurt her. And she would *never* ever want to be hit with a whip or gouged with spurs.

Andie sat bolt upright. Mary Beth's idea wasn't so dumb after all, she decided. Now she at least had a plan. And maybe, just maybe, it would work!

8

"What in the world is *this*?" Ms. Shiroo asked at inspection the next morning. She was bent over, looking under Andie's bed. Reaching underneath it, the dorm mother pulled out something brown and dusty.

Andie held her nose. "I don't know."

Mary Beth, Jina, and Lauren started to giggle.

Holding the thing gingerly with two fingers, Ms. Shiroo carried it over to a plastic trash bag she'd brought into the room and dropped it in. "Really, Andie. Get the mop from the supply closet and clean up that mess under there."

Andie nodded. When she went past Mary Beth, she had to press her lips together to keep from giggling with the others.

By the time Andie came back with the mop, Ms. Shiroo was checking out the bathroom. Andie knew it would pass inspection. It had been Jina's turn to clean it, and she liked everything perfect. Even the fluffy, gingham comforter on her bed by the door looked as if it had been starched.

"What *was* that thing?" Lauren whispered when Andie went past.

"A dead rat."

Lauren and Jina both squealed.

"It was not," Mary Beth hissed. "It was one of her dirty socks. She wore the same pair all week."

"Did not!" Andie retorted, waving the mop head threateningly toward her roommate.

"Girls!" Ms. Shiroo snapped.

Andie spun around.

"Your bathroom looks great." The dorm mother smiled briefly. "Andie, I'll check under your bed again on my way back."

"Mary Beth? Jina? Are you guys ready to go?" Lauren picked up the books off the desk beside her bed.

"Sure." Mary Beth already had her backpack slung over one shoulder.

"Me too," Jina said. Stuffing a book in her

backpack, she followed them out the door. "See you later," she said over her shoulder to Andie.

"See you," Andie muttered. Then she flattened down on the floor. Whooshing the mop under the bed, she pushed the dirt across the floor and under Lauren's bed. Lauren's pink flowery bedspread and matching dust ruffle made Andie want to puke.

Dust filled her nose and she started to sneeze. She jumped up and grabbed a tissue from the box on Jina's desk.

While she was there, Andie poked through all the riding books Jina had lined up on her desk top. *Showing Strategies*, *Top Form*, *Jumping Secrets*.

Andie shook her head in disgust. All the books were about winning.

Then her gaze settled on a paperback stuck between two other books. *Problem Horses*.

Eagerly, Andie pulled it out and flipped through the pages. Skimming the table of contents, she saw it had sections on shying and rearing.

Quickly, she closed the book and tucked it inside her history text. She could read it during her classes. Most of her teachers were rehashing boring stuff she'd covered in her last school, and the book just might have some tips she could use in her first session with Magic.

"So when the English fleets landed in New Amsterdam, how did Peter Stuyvesant react?" Ms. Thaney asked the sixth grade history class that afternoon. "Andrea?"

Andie's head snapped up, and she slammed her textbook shut on *Problem Horses*.

"Umm..." Andie stalled, trying not to look confused. Her gaze sought Mary Beth, who sat one desk up and always knew the answers.

"Chickens and hogs," Mary Beth mouthed.

"Chickens and hogs," Andie said, smiling confidently at the teacher.

Ms. Thaney's brows shot up. "Pardon me?" she said. The rest of the students burst out laughing. Someone in the corner made oinking noises.

Andie flushed red. "Uh, I meant—"

"I think you'd better pay attention, Andrea," Ms. Thaney said. "This material *will* be covered on tomorrow's quiz." She turned to the blackboard, and Andie shot Mary Beth a murderous look.

Her roommate smothered a laugh before turning around. In the front of the class, Jina and Lauren and several other sixth graders still giggled softly. And Tiffany Dubray, the snotty blonde who sat next to Andie, smirked behind her book.

"Jerks," Andie muttered. Slouching back in her chair, she tried to listen to Ms. Thaney. But her gaze kept straying to the clock on the wall. An hour and a half left to go before the riding program started. She couldn't wait.

"I've been reading up on problem horses," Andie told Mrs. Caufield later that afternoon. "And what I'd like to do with Magic is lots of grooming and walks."

"Walks?" The director raised one brow. She was leaning back in her chair, her boots propped on the top of her cluttered desk.

Andie's heart sank. She could tell the director hated her idea already.

"What will you do when he shies, pulls away from you, and bolts into the road?"

"Um," Andie stammered. She hadn't thought about that. "How about if I walk him only in enclosed areas?"

To Andie's surprise, the riding director nodded. "Okay."

"Thanks." Andie grinned. Sometimes Caufield could be okay.

As she crossed the grass-covered courtyard, she started to whistle cheerfully. Jina and Superstar had already left for their lesson with Todd. Lauren and her school horse, Whisper, were working with Katherine Parks. Mary Beth and Dangerous Dan were being led around the indoor ring.

But for once, Andie didn't mind that she wasn't riding. Another student was jumping Ranger today, so she was going to spend a whole hour with Magic.

When she reached Magic's stall, his head was down. When he heard her, it popped up, and his ears flicked back and forth nervously.

Mistake number one, Andie told herself. She should have talked to him as she was walking up.

"Okay, guy. I'm here to groom you. See?" Standing outside the stall, Andie held up one brush. He ignored it and continued chewing his hay.

Okay, so he *should* know what a brush was. But she was going to follow the advice in the

Problem Horses book anyway. Take things slow and easy. And wasn't that how she would want to be treated if she were Magic?

Next she held up the wooden grooming kit. "This is what I keep all the brushes in," she told him.

Curious, Magic stuck his head over the Dutch door and sniffed it.

"I know. It smells like other horses." Andrea set the grooming kit down and stepped closer to the stall door. "And this is me." She spread her arms wide. "I don't smell like a horse. Well, sometimes I do."

Magic's eyes widened as he snuffled her bare arms. Turning slowly, she let him sniff her back. When she was facing him again, she stooped and blew in his nostrils.

He blew back.

"That means 'Hello, I'm a friend,'" she told him as she unlatched the lower door. She walked into his stall, carrying a brush.

Andie stood for a moment staring at Magic. She'd almost forgotten how gorgeous he was—the gleaming white star, his well-muscled body, and alert expression. She reached out to pat him.

Startled, Magic wheeled clockwise so fast

that his muscular hindquarters smacked Andie in the chest. His flank hit her hard, and she flew backward like a rag doll.

With a cry of surprise, Andie hit the stable wall and slumped limply to the straw-covered floor.

Stunned, Andie sat for a moment where she had fallen. Finally, a rustling and snorting sound made her glance up sharply. Magic was huddled in the corner of his stall.

Then a pounding in the back of Andie's head made her reach around and feel under her hair.

"Ouch," she murmured, gingerly touching the lump that was already forming.

Magic eyed her suspiciously.

"It's just me," she told him. She was furious with herself. A thousand *should have*s raced through her mind. She should have been more careful. She should have talked to him.

But how was she to know? She'd never met a horse like Magic.

Maybe he *was* crazy.

Slowly, Andie leaned forward and, holding on to the side of the wall, pulled herself up. For a second, she swayed dizzily. But she didn't dare tell anyone what had happened. Caufield would never let her back in Magic's stall.

She slowly bent down and picked up the brush. When she straightened up again, her head throbbed painfully. Magic still hid in the corner.

Andie forced a grin. "Hey, dummy, you're bigger than me. Watch where you're going, okay?"

This time, she approached the horse with her hand outstretched. Talking quietly, she snapped the lead line onto his halter and brushed his right side, running over his tense muscles with the soft bristles.

When it was time to do his left side, she moved Magic away from the wall. Would he bolt again? she wondered. His head shot up, but he didn't move. Gently, Andie brushed him, singing a song while she worked, so he'd know she was there.

"Giddyap, horsie, go to town. Take care, little pony, don't fall down."

For a second, she paused. Where had she

heard such a dopey song? Maybe a long time ago, before her parents' marriage had turned into a messy divorce, her mother had sung it to her.

Andie snorted and brushed Magic harder. Her *mother*. What a joke. Old Momsie was somewhere in Europe with her latest boyfriend. Not that she could blame her mother for leaving her father. He was always working.

But did her mother have to leave her, too?

Suddenly, Andie heard the clank of horseshoes on the concrete aisle outside Magic's door.

"How's it going in there?" someone called.

Magic spun in his stall and stuck his head over the Dutch door. Lauren was standing outside, holding Whisper. She was wearing her riding helmet, schooling sweats, and high black boots. Whisper's neck was lathered with sweat.

"How's it going?" Andie echoed. "Oh, it's going great. I almost got trampled."

"You sound like Mary Beth," Lauren said, giggling. "Remember how you teased her when she thought Dan was going to stomp her to death?"

"Yeah, I do." Andie touched the lump on the back of her head. "So how was your lesson?"

"Super." Lauren beamed. Whisper was a small, chestnut mare, and the two of them looked perfect together. "Katherine's going to enter me in the dressage competition in a few weeks."

"That's cool," Andie said, feeling a twinge of envy. Lauren was going to be in her first competition, and she, Andie, would still be brushing Magic.

"Well, I'd better bathe Whisper. She's pretty hot." Clucking to the mare, Lauren led her down the aisle.

Andie turned back to Magic. "Cleaning out hooves time." She pulled the curved metal hoof pick from her pocket, and butterflies started to flutter in her stomach.

Stop it, she scolded herself. She'd never been scared to pick up a horse's foot before. But then she'd never worked with a horse as jumpy as Magic.

When she turned to face his tail, her heart raced. Standing next to his right front leg, she ran her hand down to his fetlock, the joint above the hoof. Then she bent over, her head still pounding like a relentless drum.

"Hoof," she said in a stern voice, squeezing her fingers on both sides of the joint.

Immediately, Magic picked up his foot.

Andie sighed with relief.

One down, three to go.

"Where did you get that *Practical Horseman*?" Jina asked Andie that night. All of the four roommates were in their suite for study time.

Andie flipped a page of her magazine. She lay flat on her bed, her long legs propped against the wall. "Caufield has a bunch in her office. I'm reading an article on equine massage."

"Massage?" Mary Beth almost dropped the book she was reading. "You're going to massage a *horse*?"

"You can practice on me." Lauren pushed back her desk chair and stretched her arms into the air. "This math homework is making me tense."

"I've heard of equine massage," Jina said. She was sitting on the floor, notes scattered around her. "But I thought it was for horses with sore muscles."

"It's also to relax them," Andie said.

"What about your homework?" Mary Beth asked.

Andie shrugged. "What homework?"

"Well, I know for sure you have a history quiz tomorrow," Mary Beth said. She shot a grin at Lauren and Jina. "You know—hogs and chickens?"

Andie cocked one brow. "That reminds me, Finney." She swung her legs around to the floor. "Those New Amsterdam chickens left you a little present."

"Like what?" Mary Beth asked suspiciously.

Unzipping a side pocket on her backpack, Andie pulled out something oval and white. "A rotten egg!" she answered, and threw it across the room.

Mary Beth scrambled to a kneeling position just as the egg landed with a plop on her quilt. "You jerk!"

"Ha-ha!" Andie chortled. "Don't worry, it's hard boiled."

"Ooo, it still stinks," Lauren said, holding her nose.

"Phew," Jina scooted away from Mary Beth's bed. "Get that thing out of here, Andie."

But Andie had already settled back onto the bed and was reading her magazine again. "I've got something more important to do," she said. "And it sure isn't homework," she added under her breath. She had two weeks to figure out how to calm Magic down. That wasn't much time.

The next morning, when Mary Beth's alarm rang, Andie threw her pillow at it. The clock fell to the floor with a clang.

"Hey!" Mary Beth protested, sitting up. Her red hair was sticking out every which way.

"Hey, yourself," Andie mumbled from under the blanket. *Seven o'clock. What torture.*

Lauren shot out of bed. "I get the shower first!"

"Who cares?" Andie retorted.

"You should," Jina replied as she flipped back her comforter. "We've got Morning Meeting right after breakfast, remember?"

"Great," Andie grumbled. Once a week, all the teachers got together to bore them to death with a half hour of school news.

"Well, *I* don't want to miss Morning Meeting," Mary Beth said. "They're going to tell

71

about the special trips this weekend. And Mrs. Caufield is going to announce the horse show schedule."

Andie sighed and pulled the blanket off her face. "I guess I can always take a nap while Frawley's talking."

Fifty minutes later, the four roommates gathered in the large hallway that led from Old House to the auditorium. The entryway was crowded with girls of all ages carrying backpacks. Several faculty members hovered nearby, talking to clusters of students.

Finally, Headmaster Frawley, looking hot and uncomfortable in his dark suit, appeared at the double doors and began ushering people into the auditorium.

Andie, Jina, Mary Beth, and Lauren were standing in front of the activity board, where all the different meetings, club news, and weekend activities were posted.

"Oh boy! They're showing *Family Secrets* this weekend," Andie said. "Rated G. I can't wait," she added sarcastically.

"Look at this." Lauren pointed to another notice. "Someone is selling a pair of riding boots. Size seven."

"Hey, that's my size," Mary Beth said excitedly. She had been wearing a pair of Lauren's, which were too small. "I'll go look at them this afternoon before riding."

"And there's the dean's famous red list," Jina said. She pointed up at the information board, which held academic news.

The four girls peered at the list of names. Each one was circled in red. That way everyone could see who had broken a Foxhall rule and had to see Dean Wilkes.

"I wonder if our Breakfast Club punishment is on here," Mary Beth said.

"I doubt it," Andie replied, hoisting her backpack onto her shoulder. "That was last week's news."

"But look at this," Lauren exclaimed, pointing to one of the names. "*You're* on the red list, Andie!"

10

"I'm on the red list?" Andie exclaimed in disbelief. Pushing past Lauren, she stared closer at the circled names. There it was. *Andrea Perez*.

"Why does the dean want to see you?" Mary Beth asked, frowning.

"I don't know," Andie said. "I've never met with her before." She shrugged nonchalantly. "But who cares."

"Maybe Mrs. Caufield told her about Mike Smythe complaining at the horse show," Jina suggested.

"Or maybe Frawley's still mad about the tray of food you dumped on him last week," Mary Beth said.

"Or maybe you did something else *we* don't even know about," Lauren said.

"Hey! Butt out, guys!" Andie replied

sharply. "I'll just have to make an appointment with the dean and find out. Now let's get into the auditorium before Headmonster Frawley shuts the door in our faces."

The four girls made their way into the large room and took seats in the back row. Frawley was already on the stage, talking into a hand-held microphone. Andie immediately tuned him out. Resting her head on the back of the seat, she closed her eyes and thought about Magic.

"Foxhall policy has always been that sixth grade students are not allowed to join clubs," she heard Frawley say a few minutes later. "Our staff feels strongly that first-year students need their evenings free for studying."

"That's for sure," Mary Beth murmured, next to Andie. "They give us enough work."

"Hey, there's Mr. Lyons, the gym teacher," Lauren whispered from the seat on Andie's other side.

Andie opened one eye and looked at the stage. Frawley was handing the microphone to a man dressed in a T-shirt and shorts. Whispers and a few giggles swept through the audience.

"Isn't he gorgeous?" Lauren sighed.

"You think every guy is gorgeous," Andie said in disgust. "Besides, he's married, so you'll have to stick with Todd."

"Oh," Lauren said.

Mr. Lyons cleared his throat, and Andie slumped in her seat again

"Thursday afternoon, Bracken Hall will play Mill Hall in the dorm volleyball tournament," he announced. "We hope everyone will participate."

Cheers went up in the audience. Andie rolled her eyes. Whoopee. Then she scanned the faces in the faculty section for Dean Wilkes.

She saw the dean of students leaning against the exit door, arms crossed in front of her blouse. She looked about thirty, with chin-length straight hair.

A teacher stepped forward. "I need appointments with Marjorie Jones, Betsy Amadon—" She read off a list of names.

Andie twirled her thumbs and thought about why the dean might want to see her.

She hadn't pulled any pranks all weekend. And since Magic had been at the Foxhall stables, she hadn't thought about anything else but him.

So what could it be?

Five girls in front of Andie suddenly stood up and sang "Happy Birthday" to one of the juniors, who blushed and hid her face.

Then Morning Meeting was dismissed. The four roommates filed out with the chattering crowd of girls.

"I'll walk to class with you," Mary Beth told Jina when they finally reached the hallway. "See you guys in English." She waved to Andie and Lauren.

Lauren looked over at Andie. "Want me to walk you to the dean's office?"

"Sure, why not?" Slinging her backpack over one shoulder, Andie started down the hall.

"Hey, little Sis!" someone yelled behind them.

Andie and Lauren turned. Lauren's older sister, Stephanie, was trotting down the hall toward them. Andie thought Stephanie looked like a taller version of Lauren. Long, blond hair. Great tan. Sparkling blue eyes.

But Lauren was a lot nicer.

Ashley Stewart came up behind Stephanie. Ashley was slender and petite, and Andie knew she was a really good rider.

But not good enough to beat Jinaki Williams,

Andie added to herself with a smirk.

"What's up?" Stephanie greeted them.

"Not much," Lauren replied. "I'm just walking Andie down to the dean's office."

"Oooo." Stephanie raised one brow, then nudged Ashley. "Hey, Ash, I bet Andie's going to be the bad girl of sixth grade."

"I am not," Andie retorted.

Stephanie grinned. "Just don't get my sister into trouble."

"So where's Miss Wonder Rider?" Ashley asked.

"You mean Jina?" Lauren asked.

"She's out practicing," Andie put in quickly, "so she can beat you again at the next show."

Ashley's face turned red. "Not a chance," she said. Then she grabbed Stephanie's elbow. "Come on, Steph. Let's get out of here."

"Okay. See you, Sis." Stephanie ruffled Lauren's hair, and she and Ashley took off down the hall.

"That Ashley's a snake," Andie said.

"Well, you weren't very nice either," Lauren said.

They wove through the maze of small rooms and halls until they came to an open door. Andie peered inside. A tiny, gray-haired woman was perched behind a huge wooden desk. Folds of skin hung from her neck. Glasses dangled from a silver chain.

"That's Mrs. Krabbitz, the dean's secretary," Lauren whispered.

"That fossil signed me in this summer," Andie whispered back. "Do you think she's been secretary ever since 1889, when the school started?"

Lauren smothered a giggle, and Andie was glad her roommate had offered to tag along. Not that she'd ever admit it.

"Good luck," Lauren said, waving as she left.

Andie stepped up to the desk. "Hi. My name's Andrea Perez. I'd like to make an appointment with Dean Wilkes."

Mrs. Krabbitz stuck her glasses on her nose and studied an open book. "Four o'clock. Sharp."

"Sorry, but I can't make it at four," Andie said. "I'm in the riding program."

"Four o'clock," the secretary repeated. Swiveling sideways in her chair, she began to type on a computer keyboard.

Andie stood speechless. What was she going to do? No way would she waste one precious afternoon with Magic. Finally, she walked quietly over to a chair by the wall. Mrs. Krabbitz stopped typing.

"May I help you, Ms. Perez?"

"No. I'm just waiting for Dean Wilkes."

"But I told you—"

Just then the door to the dean's office opened, and an older girl stepped out. Dean Wilkes was right behind her.

"Thank you for seeing me," the girl said.

"Anytime, Jennifer."

Clutching her backpack in front of her, Andie jumped up. "Dean Wilkes, may I see you a moment?"

"I told Ms. Perez to come at four o'clock," Mrs. Krabbitz said sternly from behind her desk.

"Please?" Andie flashed her very best smile.

The dean hesitated. "Oh, all right. You *are* on my list of students to see, I believe."

She ushered Andie into her office. Andie sat down in front of the desk and carefully crossed her legs. Her heart was pounding. When she looked up, Dean Wilkes was gazing steadily at her with deep, brown eyes.

"So you're Andrea Perez," she said finally.

Andie nodded.

"I understand you're having quite a time adjusting to Foxhall so far."

"Well—"

"In your first week here, you were given Breakfast Club for being out of the dorm after hours."

Andie opened her mouth to explain.

Dean Wilkes held up her hand. "I understand the circumstances. But you were also given kitchen cleanup for purposely dumping your food tray on Headmaster Frawley."

"Yes, but—"

"And now I'm getting reports from *all* your teachers that you are neither completing your homework nor preparing for quizzes."

Andie pretended to be surprised. "All?"

Dean Wilkes looked down at a folder on her desk and flipped through some papers. "I see you were dismissed from two other private schools last year. That's quite a record."

Andie bit her lip. This definitely wasn't going well.

"I believe I understand what is going on here." Making a steeple with her fingers, Dean Wilkes leaned forward.

Andie swallowed hard. "You do?"

"Yes." The dean raised one brow. "I believe you're trying your hardest to get kicked out of Foxhall Academy, too. And at the rate you're going, Ms. Perez, that's going to happen *very* soon."

11

"Soon?" Andie croaked. Her fingers dug into the arms of her chair.

She'd thought about this moment from the day she'd arrived at Foxhall. Getting kicked out of the other schools had been such fun. Her dad had been wonderfully furious. He'd even left work early to bring her home. Plus, she'd gotten to finish fifth grade at the neighborhood school, where no one knew her. It had been so easy to cut class and hang out at the mall.

But now, suddenly, Andie didn't think getting kicked out of Foxhall would be any fun at all. Now she had Magic to work with and Ranger to ride. Even her roommates were okay.

Tears pricked Andie's eyes. Hastily, she

wiped them away. "I didn't realize—" she said, her voice faltering.

"You didn't realize what?" Dean Wilkes said. "That you were neglecting your studies? That you were breaking rules left and right? Or"—her voice softened slightly—"that you wouldn't *want* to get kicked out of Foxhall?"

Andie's eyes filled with tears.

Dean Wilkes set down her pen. "Andie, any student who's gotten expelled from two different schools must have her reasons. I'm not sure what yours might be. But I'm going to try hard to figure out what we can do to help you. However—"

Andie tensed. Here came the big lecture.

"You're going to have to help me and the other faculty members. Your teachers turned in your name because they were worried that something was wrong. No one at Foxhall wants to see you expelled. At the same time, we can't have students who continue to break rules."

Dean Wilkes sat back in her desk chair and looked at Andie, waiting for her to respond.

"I understand." Andie slid farther down in her seat.

"Any suggestions on what we can do to

make things easier for you here?" the dean asked.

Andie shook her head.

"Well, then, there are a few things we'll need to do to get you back on track. First, Mr. Jackson, your study-skills teacher, is going to sit down with you and draw up a homework chart. Second, I'm going to call your father and set up a meeting."

Andie inhaled sharply. "My father?"

Dean Wilkes nodded. "For Thursday."

"Good luck," Andie mumbled.

"If the chart doesn't work, you'll be given supervised study hall. Do you know what that is?"

Andie nodded. *Jail.* Every night during study time, she'd be confined to a small room at Old House, where a teacher would hang over her shoulder.

"In the meantime," Dean Wilkes continued, "I will be receiving daily reports from your teachers. You'll meet with me every morning to discuss them."

Great, Andie thought.

"So I will see you tomorrow morning. Please make your appointment with Mrs. Krabbitz on your way out."

"Thank you." Andie stood up, and then she made a dash for the door.

Mrs. Krabbitz held out a late pass. Andie grabbed it as she raced past, calling, "I need another appointment—for Wednesday—seven forty-five." She didn't wait for an answer. She was too upset.

Andie sprinted down the hallway to an exit door. It led to the garden behind Old House.

When she got outside, she looked around. No one else was in the flower-filled garden.

Andie leaned back against the door, her mind spinning. Was Dean Wilkes right? Did she really want to stay at Foxhall?

I might as well face it, Andie told herself. What was there for her to do at home? Her dad was always at work, she didn't know any of the kids in the neighborhood, and Maria was just a hired housekeeper.

Besides, public school had tons of rules, too. At least there was a riding program at Foxhall—and Magic.

So if I want to stay, why do I keep messing up?

Andie pressed her fingers against her pounding head. Dean Wilkes had said that if she wanted to stay at Foxhall, she'd have to follow a homework chart, have daily progress meetings, and sit through an interview with her father.

Andie moaned. How had things gone so wrong?

Sliding down the door, she buried her head in her arms and began to sob.

That afternoon, Jina, Andie, and Lauren cheered and whistled as they watched Mary Beth's lesson. She was trotting for the first time!

Andie held Magic firmly by the lead line. He was nervously watching what was going on in the ring.

Hooked to a longe line, Dangerous Dan was jogging around and around in small circles. He was a huge half-draft horse, and his plate-sized hooves kicked up puffs of dust with every step.

Dorothy Germaine was holding the end of the longe line. Alternately she clucked to Dan and called instructions to Mary Beth.

"Up, down. Up, down. Don't let your fanny hit the saddle so hard. The second it touches, push yourself up. Come on, Dan, don't fall asleep on me."

Her face red as a beet, Mary Beth bounced

and jostled in the saddle as she tried to post. Occasionally, she got the rhythm right and rose and fell to the beat of the trot.

"Whoa, Dan!" Dorothy called finally, and the enormous chestnut horse stopped dead in his tracks. Mary Beth lurched forward, grabbing a handful of mane just in time.

"She did it!" Lauren cried.

Andie was doubtful. "Well...she did an awful lot of bouncing."

"I didn't mean she *posted*, exactly," Lauren explained. "But she did trot. And look, she's wearing her new boots—the ones she bought from that girl who advertised on the bulletin board. I think she's ready to be a rider."

"Well, maybe," Jina said, echoing Andie's doubt.

"You two are such pessimists." Lauren put her hands on her hips. "I think we should celebrate. I'll buy some candy bars from the Snackery, Andie can get some soda—"

"Can't," Andie cut in. "I've got cleanup duty in the cafeteria. Remember?"

"Oh, right." Lauren chewed on her lip.

Jina smiled sympathetically at Andie. "I guess after that meeting with Dean Wilkes, you don't feel much like celebrating."

"Then how about a party during study hall?" Lauren suggested. "We'll shut the door. No one needs to know."

Andie sighed. "I can't then, either. The homework chart Mr. Jackson and I made up doesn't leave two seconds for anything other than studying."

"Hey, guys!" Mary Beth called. "How'd I do?"

Andie, Jina, and Lauren turned toward the gate. Mary Beth was leading Dan from the ring. Her face was streaked with dirt and sweat, but she was grinning broadly.

"You were great. We're going to have a party later to celebrate." Lauren slapped her hard on the back.

Mary Beth grimaced. "Ouch. Don't do that. Every bone in my body has been bounced lose."

Andie laughed. "Don't worry, Finney. It gets easier the more you practice."

"At least it's *supposed* to," Jina added.

Everyone laughed. Magic snorted at Dan, then pranced away from the big horse.

"Whoa," Andie told him firmly, then sighed again. "I keep telling myself this is going to get easier. See you guys later," she added, and clucking to Magic, she led him back to the pasture.

When she turned the Thoroughbred out into the field, she hung over the gate for a while and watched him greet Jake with whiffles of excitement. Andie felt a little better. At least Magic liked *someone*. Not that she'd been such great company this afternoon. But then again, it hadn't been much of a day.

She'd totally blown the history quiz, and she had a personal homework chart that looked like a bus schedule. Magic didn't seem to care if she was around or not, a new girl was riding Ranger this week, and her roommates were going to have a party without her.

Maybe it would be a lot easier if she *did* get kicked out of Foxhall.

That evening, Andie tried to relax as the warm water from the shower sprinkled on her face. It was after nine o'clock, and she'd actually studied for two whole hours.

Turning off the water, she stepped from the stall, dried off, and wrapped her terry robe around her shivering body. As she towel-dried her hair, she thought about her father. Dean Wilkes had left a note that he was definitely coming on Thursday. Andie could picture his face—red with anger at having to attend one more meeting to talk about her misbehavior.

But at least he was coming.

"You sure are feeling sorry for yourself," she told her steamy image in the mirror. Picking up her shower kit, she opened the bathroom door. The lights in the suite were out.

"Hey, guys, are you asleep already?" she asked the dark room.

There was no answer.

Suddenly, the lights switched on. Jina popped up from under her quilt, Mary Beth jumped out of the wardrobe, and Lauren emerged from behind the desk.

"Surprise!" they yelled, waving their arms excitedly. And for the second time that day, Andie started to cry.

12

"Party! Party! Party!" Jina, Mary Beth, and Lauren chanted as they began to pull sodas and snacks from under beds and out of drawers.

Quickly, Andie wiped her tears. "What's going on?" she asked.

"It's our celebration, remember?" Lauren said. "To congratulate Mary Beth for trotting a horse—"

"And not falling off," Jina chimed in as she screwed the top off several sodas.

"And to congratulate *you*—" Lauren poked her finger into Andie's chest "—on actually doing some homework."

"You jerks." Andie laughed. And she'd thought they were going to have a party without her!

"Here." Mary Beth handed her a jar of peanuts. "Start eating," she mumbled, her mouth full of chips. "We don't have much time before Shiroo comes by for lights-out."

The four girls sat cross-legged on Andie's bed. Mary Beth wore her baby doll pajamas with the poodles on them, Jina had on her nightshirt, Lauren wore a pink nightie, and Andie had on her terry robe.

"Your dad's coming Thursday, right?" Mary Beth said to Andie, licking salt off her fingers.

Andie frowned. "How'd you know that?"

"I read the message on the wipe-off board."

Andie shoveled a handful of M&Ms into her mouth. "Well, so what if he is?"

"You don't seem too happy about it," Jina said.

"Well, would *you* be happy if the dean called *your* parents?" Andie retorted.

"Hey!" Lauren clapped her hands together. "Let's play What I Like and What I Hate About My Parents."

"That sounds dumb," Jina said.

"No, it's fun, really," Lauren said excitedly. "I'll start."

She leaned back against the headboard and thought for a moment. "What I like about my dad is the way he says, 'You want a new Walkman, sugar? You'll have to earn the money to pay for it.'" She giggled. "Then he'll pay me thirty-five bucks for washing his car!"

Mary Beth stopped chewing. "I'd have to baby-sit for four years to earn that much money."

Lauren bit her lip. "All right, then. What do you like about your parents?"

"Ummm." Mary Beth cocked her head. "My mom makes great cookies."

"Yeah," Andie agreed. "I wish she'd send us more."

"Okay. Now let's do the 'hates,'" Lauren went on.

"That's easy," Mary Beth said. "I hate when my mom calls me Bethie like I'm two years old."

"Your turn, Andie," Lauren said. "What do you hate about your mother or father?"

"Everything," Andie said flatly, even if it wasn't true. "Jina's right. This *is* a dumb game." Then she pointed to her blanket. "Hey, you slobs are getting crumbs everywhere."

"Don't worry about it," Mary Beth said. "There's already enough food under your bed to feed ten mice."

Lauren turned to Jina, who was gathering up crumpled wrappers and bags. "How about you, Jina? You're the only one who hasn't said anything."

Jina flushed and jumped off the bed. "I've got to finish studying," she said.

Andie, Mary Beth, and Lauren exchanged glances as Jina walked over to her desk. Andie couldn't remember Jina ever mentioning her parents. *But,* she reminded herself, *I don't like to talk about my parents, either.*

"Well, I guess the party's over," Mary Beth said.

"Yeah." Andie finished the last of her soda, then burped loudly. "But it sure was fun while it lasted."

There was definitely something wrong with Magic, Andie finally decided. It was Thursday afternoon, and she was leaning back against the stall door, watching him.

He was watching her, too, but only with his right eye.

She'd noticed it yesterday. When she approached him from the left, he was instantly wary, even if she spoke to him. And now that she thought about it, when Magic had dumped Katherine that day, the noisy van had been on his left side, too.

What was going on?

Suddenly, Andie checked her watch. She'd been so busy thinking about Magic, she'd forgotten about the time. And she was supposed to be in Dean Wilkes's office—right now!

Dropping her brushes in the grooming kit, Andie shut the stall door and sprinted from the barn. She wouldn't have time to change. And both her father and Dean Wilkes would be furious that she was late.

Halfway down the hill to Old House, Andie slowed to a walk. So what if she was late? She didn't care what her father thought.

When she arrived, Mrs. Krabbitz frowned at her over her glasses. "You're late," she said. "Your father's already with the dean."

Andie smoothed her wild hair back behind her shoulders. Then she changed her mind and shook her head, letting her hair fly everywhere.

When she stepped into Dean Wilkes's office, the dean greeted her coolly. Her father, somber in his dark gray suit, raised one bushy brow. He had Andie's coloring, except his black hair was neatly combed, and his tan skin was etched with wrinkles.

"Hi, Dad," Andie said. Sauntering in, she slumped down in the chair next to his.

"Hello, Andrea," he replied in a formal voice. "I see you're right on time, as usual."

Andie tensed. She could tell from her father's tone that he was really mad.

"So, where were we?" Mr. Perez turned back to Dean Wilkes. "You mentioned a home-work chart."

Half an hour later, the dean and her father finished discussing her. Her father hadn't looked at her once. Andie had nodded and answered politely, hoping Dean Wilkes would notice how hard she was trying, but inside she was starting to steam.

Her father was totally ignoring her!

By the time they left the dean's office, he still hadn't looked at her.

"Would you like to see the dorm before you leave?" Andie asked him when they were out-side.

"I'm afraid I haven't time," her father said, glancing at his watch. "Though I would like to take a few minutes to speak with you."

Andie let out her breath. Oh boy. "Well, the common room in the dorm is usually empty this time of the day. Everyone's finishing up with their clubs or sports programs."

He nodded once. "Good."

Silently, they strode across the courtyard. Andie wondered if her father would give her the standard lecture. The one he'd used so many times since her parents had divorced a year ago.

Why won't you work harder at school? Why are you such a disappointment to me? Why, why, why?

"Soda?" she asked when they reached the common room.

Her father shook his head as he surveyed the worn but comfortable room.

"It's not exactly like your chrome and glass office," Andie said. "Where you chew out your employees."

He faced her then, his bushy brows joined together in a scowl. "I've had enough of your bad manners, young lady. Not only were you late, but you didn't bother to change your dirty clothes after you left the stable. And I'm sure you were ignoring everything Dean Wilkes and I discussed."

"No, I wasn't ignoring you," Andie said

angrily. "It's just that you're so used to everyone *jumping* at your command. Maybe that's the problem. You want me to salute like one of your employees!"

Mr. Perez stepped forward, shaking one finger. "The problem is your attitude, Andrea. Do you want this to be the third school you've been kicked out of?"

Andie just shrugged. She was too angry to care.

"Well, according to Dean Wilkes, who seems to be doing everything possible to help you, you're already headed in that direction. And if you do get expelled, then that's it."

"What will you do then?" Andie demanded. "Fire me?"

Mr. Perez threw up his arms. "I give up, Andrea. You used to be such a good kid. What happened?"

Suddenly, all Andie's anger bubbled to the surface. "You really don't know, do you? But since you're asking—for the first time, I might add—I'll tell you.

"I *used* to try to be perfect. Because I was so afraid that if I wasn't, you and Mom would hate each other even more, and you'd get a divorce."

She glared up into his dark eyes. "Only my being perfect didn't matter. You got divorced anyway. Mom left to find herself, or whatever she calls it, and you work so much that the only grown-ups I see are teachers, maids, and camp counselors. So now I don't care what you think."

Spinning on her boots, Andie marched to the door of the common room. "So good-bye, Daddy-o. And quit worrying. I'll make it at Foxhall, but it won't be because *you* want me to. It'll be because it's what *I* want to do!"

Andie blasted through the double doors of Bracken Hall and sprinted across the courtyard. Tears stung her eyes.

"I hate him," she muttered angrily as she ran through the stone arch. *"Hate* him!" Hair flying behind her like a wild horse's mane, she raced up the hill toward the stable.

Andie ran past girls in rumpled riding clothes, their helmets under their arms. At the top of the hill, she dashed past Lauren and Mary Beth. Her roommates turned to stare after her.

"Hey!" Lauren called. "What's wrong?"

Andie didn't answer. She kept running until she reached the stable courtyard, where she stopped to catch her breath. A lead line was hanging over a stall door. Andie glanced around. All the students had gone. Dorothy and the other instructors were probably in Mrs. Caufield's office.

She grabbed the lead line just as Lauren and Mary Beth ran up.

"What are you doing?" Lauren asked breathlessly.

"Getting Magic," Andie replied. She walked down the aisle and around the stable to the back pasture.

"But students aren't supposed to be here now," Mary Beth said as she and Lauren jogged behind. "The riding program's over for the day."

"I know," Andie said, pushing open the pasture gate. "And I don't care. So go away."

Lauren stopped at the pasture fence. "What's wrong with you, Andie? Did you and your dad have a fight?"

Andie's fingers tightened around the lead line. Why wouldn't her roommates ever leave her alone? Staring straight ahead, she marched across the pasture.

Magic lifted his head when he saw her and nickered a greeting. He recognized her!

Holding out her hand, Andie walked up to

his right side. She snapped the lead line onto his halter, then buried her head in his neck.

"Andie? What are you doing?" Lauren called. She and Mary Beth were anxiously watching her from the fence.

Andie ignored them.

Magic moved forward until his sleek side was right in front of her. All she had to do was jump onto his back.

But Caufield had told her not to ride him.

Andie clenched her teeth. She was tired of everyone telling her what to do. They didn't care about *her*. All they cared about were their stupid rules.

Grabbing Magic's mane with her right hand, Andie flung herself onto his back. Startled, the horse stepped forward. She clung to his mane, then slid her left leg over his other side.

"Andie, no!" Lauren and Mary Beth hollered. "Don't do it!" But their voices sounded very far away.

Using the lead line like a rein, Andie steered Magic to the right. His walk was smooth and flowing. It felt so good to be riding again.

I'll just walk around for a minute, Andie told herself. *Then I'll jump off. Caufield will never even know.*

The sun was setting behind the trees and a cool breeze ruffled Andie's hair. Magic strode confidently to the far side of the pasture toward a grove of trees. *Katherine was right*, Andie thought. Magic was light and sensitive. He'd be worth all the time she was spending with him.

Suddenly, a pheasant burst from the brush to their left. Magic reared, then twisted sideways.

Andie flew off. *Wham!* She landed on her side on the ground. Quickly, she scrambled to her feet, ignoring the dull pain in her hip. Magic raced across the field toward the gate, lead line dangling.

Andie looked over at her roommates and gasped. Lauren and Mary Beth were perched on the railing—and right by the gate, a murderous expression on her face, stood Mrs. Caufield.

Mrs. Caufield opened the gate and grabbed Magic's lead line. Without a word, she led him toward the stable. When she disappeared around the corner, Mary Beth and Lauren jumped off the fence and ran toward Andie.

Lauren grabbed her arm. "Are you all right?"

Andie nodded slowly, then bent down and brushed off her dirty jeans. "Sure. The fall didn't hurt. It's knowing what Caufield's going to do that's going to hurt."

"Why did you get on Magic?" Mary Beth moaned. "You know what Caufield said."

Andie gave one last slap to her pants. "I know."

Lauren and Mary Beth glanced at each other, then looked back at Andie.

"Does this have something to do with that meeting with your dad?" Lauren asked.

Andie didn't answer.

"You know Caufield's rules are to keep all the students and horses safe," Mary Beth added.

"Maybe it does have to do with my dad," Andie said finally as she started toward the gate. "I just don't know anymore."

The three girls walked from the pasture in silence. When they reached the courtyard, Mrs. Caufield was nowhere in sight. But Andie noticed a crack of light under her office door.

She sighed. She knew she had to apologize. Not that an apology would keep her from getting kicked out of the riding program—and probably out of Foxhall, too. But she'd done something stupid that could have hurt her or Magic, and she needed to tell Caufield she was sorry.

"You guys better go and get ready for dinner," Andie told Lauren and Mary Beth as she walked slowly to the office.

"Are you sure you don't want us to stay?" Mary Beth asked.

Andie nodded. "I'll see you back at the dorm." Then she took a deep breath and knocked on Mrs. Caufield's door.

There was no answer. Turning the knob, she opened the door a little and peered in. "Mrs. Caufield?"

The director wasn't in, but a steaming cup of coffee told Andie she would be back any minute.

Besides, Mrs. Caufield had an open-door policy. If you had a problem, you could wait to see her.

Andie walked in, slumped into the beat-up chair in front of the director's desk, and thought about what she'd done. She hadn't realized how angry she'd been since her parents' divorce. And how much trouble that anger had gotten her into. Now it was probably too late to tell anyone she was sorry.

While she waited, Andie scanned the book titles arranged between the horse-head bookends on Mrs. Caufield's desk. One of the books in the middle immediately caught her eye—*Medical Answers for Horses with Problems*. Quickly, she looked through the index for "shying."

When she turned to the section, it listed different behaviors and what medical problem they might relate to. Andie's heart raced as she read:

BEHAVIOR:
1. Startles or kicks when approached on a particular side.
2. May run into objects on that side.
3. Refuses to cross over or jump ditches or strange objects.
4. Unusually fearful when encountering new situations.
5. May have experienced a recent accident or suffered injury to the head.

That described Magic perfectly! Eagerly,

Andie kept reading.

If your horse demonstrates more than one of the above behaviors, consider that he may have a problem with the sight in one or both of his eyes. For example, if your horse has a detached retina, his eye would appear normal and the animal would experience no pain. Only a complete ophthalmic exam would reveal this type of trauma.

The sudden slamming of the office door made Andie jump. Arms crossed, lips pressed in a line, Mrs. Caufield looked down at her.

But Andie barely noticed the director's angry expression. She jumped up and waved the open book excitedly.

"I found it!" she cried. "I found out what's wrong with Magic!"

14

For a moment, the director seemed startled by Andie's outburst. Then she frowned. "Andrea, you obviously don't realize the trouble you're in."

"Yes, I do." Andie nodded. "But I don't care right now. I mean, I do, but I want you to listen to this. I think it will help Magic."

Without waiting for a response, Andie started reading from the book. When she was finished, the director was tapping her cheek with one finger as if she'd listened to every word.

Andie closed the book and held her breath.

"You know," Mrs. Caufield said finally, "you may have something there. Magic's owner isn't a real horsewoman. Oh, she loves horses and has lots of money to buy them, but I'm sure she relies on trainers to tell her what to do."

Still tapping her cheek, the director began to pace the room. "If that trailer accident caused an injury to Magic's eye, she probably wouldn't have picked it up. I remember she said Magic seemed unhurt, so they didn't call a vet. And—" swinging around, she faced Andie with an excited expression "—Magic's had a slew of trainers since then, so they might not have noticed the problem, either."

Mrs. Caufield grabbed a lead line from a hook on the wall and started out the door. "Come on, Andie. I know a simple test to find out if he can't see in one eye. Which eye did you say it was?"

"The left." Excitedly, Andie followed the director out of the office and across the court-yard to Magic's stall.

When they reached the stall, Mrs. Caufield swung open the door. Surprised, Magic flung his head up and stepped sideways—right into the wall.

Mrs. Caufield shook her head. "I should have wondered more about his odd behavior, instead of calling him crazy," she said softly.

Snapping the lead line on Magic's halter, she pulled the horse around until his left eye was facing the dim light from the aisle.

"Okay, Andie. You watch and tell me if Magic blinks or flinches."

Andie nodded. The director moved around to Magic's right side, talking to him in a soothing voice. Next she moved her hand under his throat to his left cheek and wiggled her fingers in front of his left eye.

Andie gasped. "He didn't even know your fingers were there."

"Well, then, Ms. Perez, I think you may be right," Mrs. Caufield said, ducking under the horse's head. "I'll call the vet first thing in the morning. Then we'll find out for sure what's going on with Mr. Magic."

"If it *is* something like a detached retina, can it be fixed?" Andie asked worriedly.

"Well..." Mrs. Caufield hesitated. "I'm not sure. It's been a long time since that trailer accident."

Andie sucked in her breath. "That doesn't sound good."

Mrs. Caufield squeezed her shoulder reassuringly. "Let's wait and see what the vet says." Unsnapping the lead line, she headed out of the stall.

Andie took one last look at Magic, then followed the director into the aisle. "Uh, Mrs. Caufield," she began hesitantly. "I think I have some explaining to do."

The director nodded curtly. "And I'm ready to hear your explanation."

"But first I want to apologize," Andie said. "I'm sorry for getting on Magic. He could have gotten hurt."

"And *you* could have been hurt, too, Andie," the director pointed out.

"I know. I'm not even sure why I did it." Tears stung Andie's eyes. She sniffled and wiped her cheeks with the back of her hand. "I guess I've just been mad about stuff for a long time. And breaking rules was my way of getting back at everybody. I know that's no excuse, but—"

"Look, Andie," Mrs. Caufield broke in. "Dean Wilkes and I have talked about you many times. We were both hoping your interest in horses would keep you on the right track at Foxhall. So far, it hasn't seemed to have worked."

Andie's head snapped up. "Oh, but this week I *have* been trying. And I'll try harder."

The director smiled faintly. "Personally, I think you *are* trying. I'm really proud of your patience with Magic. But I'm not the only person you'll have to convince. Foxhall Academy is not just about horses. It's about getting a good education. And that means homework and tests and all that goes with it. Right?"

"Right." Andie nodded solemnly. "And I do want to stay at Foxhall, Mrs. Caufield. Honest," she added, surprised to hear herself actually saying it.

Slowly, she started to grin. There, she'd said it out loud: *I want to stay at Foxhall*.

It felt really good to say it.

On Friday afternoon Andie stood nervously in Magic's stall, holding the horse for the veterinarian. "Yup, it's a detached retina all right," Dr. Holden said when he'd completed his examination with the ophthalmoscope.

Mrs. Caufield nodded from where she was standing against the wall. Jina, Mary Beth, and Lauren were just outside, hanging over the stall door.

Andie patted Magic's lathered neck. Considering he'd had such an audience during the exam, she thought he'd behaved great.

"Actually, the retina is just partially detached, the top folding onto the bottom,"

Dr. Holden explained as he stuck the ophthal-moscope in his coverall pocket. "So Magic *can* be operated on. That's the good news."

"The bad news is the operation costs an arm and a leg, right?" Mrs. Caufield said.

The vet nodded. "Right. And there's always a chance the operation may not work," he added.

Andie swallowed hard.

Mrs. Caufield must have noticed her expression. Reaching over, she squeezed Andie's arm. "I'll do everything I can, Andie. But I have to be frank with you. The school doesn't have money for an operation like this. And even if Magic does recover his sight, I'm afraid he still may not be a good horse for the school."

Andie pressed her lips together, trying hard to keep from crying. "So what's going to happen to him?"

"I'll give him back to his original owner. But don't worry. I'm sure she'll see that he gets the right care."

Give him back! Andie stood stunned as Mrs. Caufield followed Dr. Holden from the stall. She couldn't believe it. Hadn't the director told her just yesterday how very proud she was that Andie had taken such an interest in Magic?

And now they were getting rid of him anyway!

"Andie, are you all right?" someone asked. Andie snapped her head around. Jina, Mary Beth, and Lauren were hovering around the stall door, staring at Andie with worried expressions.

"I can't believe it!" Andie said angrily. "Caufield's getting rid of him. They all make decisions and they just don't care! They don't care what I think!"

Sobbing, she spun around and buried her head in Magic's neck.

The stall door opened as Andie's roommates hurried in. Magic looked at them suspiciously, but he didn't move. Lauren threw an arm around Andie's shoulders. No one said anything.

"Grown-ups really can be jerks," Mary Beth finally blurted out.

"Look, guys," Jina interrupted. "Instead of feeling sorry for ourselves, let's figure out how to keep Magic here."

"What are you talking about?" Andie asked, lifting up her head.

Jina looked down at the floor. "Well, my mom's busy a lot, too, and I don't have a dad," she said. "But that's not always bad. It means I have to be responsible for myself a lot."

"So what's your idea?" Andie asked.

Jina flushed. "I don't really have an idea. It's just that if I were in this situation, I'd think, Okay, Jina, what can you do to get what you want?"

"Well, what I want is Magic," Andie said.

"Gee," Lauren chimed in. "If I want something, I just ask my parents for it. I don't always get it, but sometimes I do. Why don't you ask your dad to buy Magic? Then you could board him at Foxhall."

Andie shook her head. "Great idea, guys, but after our big blowout yesterday, my dad probably won't even talk to me."

"Andie!" someone hollered outside the stall door.

Lauren turned and called, "She's in here!"

Katherine Parks came up and leaned over the door. "You've got company," she said.

"Company?" Andie repeated, puzzled.

Stepping past Lauren and Jina, she made her way to the open door. A man wearing a short-sleeved knit shirt, jeans, and tennis shoes was standing in the middle of the courtyard. He was looking curiously at the girls riding past on their horses.

Andie caught her breath.

"Who is it?" Mary Beth asked, looking over Andie's shoulder.

"I don't believe it," Andie said. "It's my *father!*"

15

Andie ran into the courtyard. "What are *you* doing here?" she asked.

Her father turned around, a hesitant smile on his lips. Andie hadn't seen him dressed casually in a long time. He looked really different.

"I thought we might have dinner together."

"*Dinner?*" The word stuck in Andie's throat.

Mr. Perez nodded. "Yes. If you'd like, your roommates could come along, too," he added, running his fingers nervously through his graying hair. "I've gotten permission for them already. All they need to do is fill in the Sign-Out Book."

Andie glanced over her shoulder. Jina, Lauren, and Mary Beth were hanging around Magic's stall. They were pretending not to be interested in what was going on.

"That sounds neat. I'll ask them," Andie replied uncertainly. She had no idea why her father was here. He never came to school on his own. "We'll all have to get cleaned up first."

"No problem." Mr. Perez smiled, then looked around again. "So this is where you ride."

"Right." Andie shoved her hands in her jeans pockets, feeling awkward. Why was her father so interested all of a sudden?

Her father dropped his gaze. "Andie, I want to apologize."

Andie was stunned. *"Apologize?"*

"I called Dean Wilkes this morning. She told me you've really been trying since she met with you on Tuesday. And as for your outburst after our meeting, well, you told me some things that I needed to hear."

He cleared his throat and scuffed some grass with his feet. "You see, Andie, when your mother and I divorced, we were both caught up in our own problems. I'm afraid we didn't realize how much it was hurting you." His voice broke. "I'm sorry."

Tears welled up in Andie's eyes, but she quickly bit them back. She couldn't believe her father was apologizing. And she had no idea what to say.

"Do you want to meet my roommates?" she asked finally.

"Sure."

Side by side, they walked over to Magic's stall. Andie had never noticed how tall and lean her father was. Maybe it was because his suits made him look like a stuffy old banker.

As Andie introduced Jina, Mary Beth, and Lauren, her father shook hands with each of them. Then Jina nudged Andie with her elbow.

"What?" Andie said.

"You forgot to introduce Magic." Jina nodded toward Magic's stall. His head was hanging over the door as he curiously watched the group.

"Oh, right," she said. She turned to her father and cleared her throat. "Dad, I need you to meet one more person. I mean, he's not a person, he's a horse, but—"

"He's very important to Andie," Mary Beth chimed in.

"And we're sure that when you hear his *sad* story, you'll want to help," Lauren added.

Mr. Perez raised his eyebrows. "Are all you

girls ganging up on me?" he asked, his voice serious.

"Well—" Andie flushed.

Her father suddenly grinned. "Hey, I do business with some sharp guys. But I have a feeling you four are going to give me a run for my money." He crossed his arms and looked at the girls.

"So let's hear it."

At seven the next morning, the stable was bustling with activity. Andie, Lauren, and Mary Beth had awoken early to help Jina and the other riders get ready for Saturday's show.

Andie was sitting on the tack room floor cleaning a bridle, but she couldn't concentrate. Her father had spent the night in town. Now he was in the office, talking to Mrs. Caufield about Magic. Last night, he'd said he'd make a decision after he spoke to the director.

"Lauren told me I'd find you here," a deep voice said.

Andie looked up. Her father was standing in the doorway.

Dropping the sponge and bridle, she jumped to her feet. "So, did you meet with

Mrs. Caufield already, Dad?"

He nodded.

"And?" Andie crossed her fingers.

"Well, I've weighed all the risks. And you know, Andrea, there are plenty of risks in the horse business." He frowned. "And even more of them with Magic, since he has to have that operation."

"*Dad!*" Andie protested. "You're talking about a living, breathing thing, not buying shares of stock."

"I know. And I also know you really care about the horse. So Mrs. Caufield suggested we lease Magic. That means I would pay the vet bills—including for the operation—shoeing, and board. And *you* get to ride him. How does that sound?"

For a moment, Andie felt disappointed.

"I know you'd rather own him." Her father touched her lightly on the arm. "But let's take things one step at a time. We'll lease Magic on a temporary basis and see how the operation goes. Meanwhile, I'm going to meet with Dean Wilkes every week to check on your grades and behavior. If you work hard the rest of this semester, we'll see about buying the horse."

"Do you really mean it?" Andie asked, clapping her hands.

"Do we have a deal?" her father countered.

"We have a deal!" Jumping up, Andie gave him a quick hug, then sprinted out the tack room door.

Girls and horses turned to stare at her as she raced across the courtyard to Magic's stall.

"What happened?" Mary Beth called out running up with Lauren. They'd been helping Jina braid her horse. Jina jogged down the aisle, too, leading Superstar.

Throwing open Magic's stall door, Andie rushed in and threw her arms around the horse's neck.

"He's mine! All mine!"

A low chuckle told Andie that her father had followed her from the tack room. He was standing outside the stall with her roommates.

"Well, girls, Magic's not exactly Andie's," she heard him explain. "We're going to lease him this semester."

"That's great!" Lauren and Mary Beth said together.

"Congratulations, Andie," Jina added. "He's a terrific horse."

"And he's mine, mine, mine," Andie

chanted. She didn't care what her father said.

Everyone laughed. Finally, Andie gave Magic one last hug, then turned toward the group standing by the stall door. Grinning from ear to ear, she glanced from Lauren to her dad to Jina, then over to Mary Beth. She couldn't remember the last time she'd felt this happy.

Okay, so the next couple of weeks were going to be rough. Homework charts, meetings with Dean Wilkes, kitchen detail—all those *rules*.

Would it be worth it?

Then Andie's gaze caught her dad's, and they grinned at each other. When she turned back to Magic, he was staring at her with his big brown eyes.

It would *definitely* be worth it.

"Let's go, guys," she told Lauren and Mary Beth happily. "It's time to get Jina ready for the horse show. She's got a championship to win!"

Don't miss the next book
in the Riding Academy series:
#3: JINA RIDES TO WIN

Don't panic! Jina told herself. *Think!*

The fence was looming in front of them. She tried to collect Superstar, but it was too late. She signaled the horse to take off, even though she knew they were too far back.

Win a big one for me. Jina heard her mother's words echoing in her head. *Win!*

Superstar flew over the fence, and Jina's heart leaped with him. Maybe they'd be okay.

But the gray dapple's hind leg caught the top rail, and he landed awkwardly. Head down, he stumbled forward. Jina grabbed a braid and held tight. Like the well-trained horse he was, Superstar caught himself before he fell.

Gamely, the horse began to canter toward the fifth fence. But Jina realized immediately that something was wrong. His rhythm was way off.

Superstar was hurt. And it was all her fault!

**If you love horses, you'll enjoy
these other books from Bullseye:**

THE BLACK STALLION
THE BLACK STALLION RETURNS
THE BLACK STALLION AND THE GIRL
SON OF THE BLACK STALLION
A SUMMER OF HORSES
WHINNY OF THE WILD HORSES